THE KILLINGS AT BARLEY HALL

THE KILLINGS AT BARLEY HALL

Barbara Whitehead

Chivers Press   •   Thorndike Press
Bath, England   Thorndike, Maine USA

This Large Print edition is published by Chivers Press, England, and by Thorndike Press, USA.

Published in 1997 in the U.K. by arrangement with Constable & Company.

Published in 1997 in the U.S. by arrangement with Teresa Chris Literary Agency.

U.K. Hardcover   ISBN   0–7451–6995–3   (Chivers Large Print)
U.K. Softcover   ISBN   0–7451–6996–1   (Camden Large Print)
U.S. Softcover   ISBN   0–7862–0960–7   (General Series Edition)

The text of this Large Print edition is unabridged.
Other aspects of the book may vary from the original edition.

Set in 16 pt. New Times Roman.

Printed in Great Britain on acid-free paper.

British Library Cataloguing in Publication Data available

Library of Congress Catalog Card Number: 96–90800

*With thanks to the York Archaeological Trust
for their help and co-operation.*

CHAPTER ONE

It was nearing twelve o'clock on a Wednesday night in the centre of the city of York, and Police Constable John Clark was on foot patrol. Wednesday night was usually fairly peaceful, whereas Thursday night was a bit iffy. Not like Friday or Saturday, when the patrol was in teams of two, but a bit iffy all the same. As he left the lights of St Sampson's Square behind him and headed down an unfrequented side alley by the light of his torch, Clark was glad that it was still only Wednesday.

In many ways he loved night patrol. There were unexpected places and quiet corners in the heart of the old walled city which came into their own in the peaceful depths of the night. Then only the moon and stars shone fitfully from the sky into the complex townscape of pantiled roofs and narrow winding roads and intersecting pathways and courtyards. Lower than the stars, most of the street lamps along the thoroughfares were alight all night. Here and there down the old footways lamps were fixed by brackets, illuminating a few yards before the blackness returned in the shadows of the brick walls.

The pubs were shut so there was no light from there. The central tower of the floodlit

1

cathedral glowed against the night sky, then suddenly went dark. Clark shone his torch on to his wrist and looked at his watch. Midnight. The floodlighting on beautiful buildings throughout York would all be going out now. Time clocks would be clicking off the illumination from shop windows. The city from midnight to dawn was more like its ancient self than at any other time, magical, mysterious.

A large white cat, fluffy and ghostlike, appeared on top of a yard wall, then leapt across the four or five feet to the opposite wall, flying soundlessly through the air over PC Clark's head. If there was nothing worse than the shock that gave him, he wouldn't mind. He might even settle to enjoy the next few hours. Most of the drunks should have cleared by now. There were few cars. Those passing through the city were heard individually through the calm air, traced by sound alone.

He was now moving to another alleyway, Coffee Yard, which led from Back Swinegate to Stonegate, going through buildings and across courtyards. There was a wall lamp at the Swinegate end, and another fixed on the wall of Thomas Gent's Coffee House at the Stonegate end, but in between there were great pools of shadow and black areas. Clark swung the beam of his torch from side to side, idly noticing fag ends and screwed-up paper bags and other kinds of rubbish. Not many people could have had mothers like his. She went crazy if he left litter on the ground. He would feel guilty even now if he dropped anything.

After threading his way through a low covered-in part of the alley, Clark came out into the dark courtyard where all that building work was going on. The next lamp only lit part of this. He swung his torch round, to check if the place was clear of drunks, and to see how the builders had got on since he was here yesterday.

There was something over there at the other side of the yard that shouldn't be there. John Clark crossed the courtyard, sure he was on the way to finding a drunk sleeping it off on the rough ground. But step by step as he went he changed his mind. He felt a steely calm flood over him. It was then that Clark discovered how he reacted to shock. He'd often wondered how he'd shape up to a situation like this. Even before he came to a stop beside the man, who was lying on his back, Clark knew that this man was dead, even before he noticed the blood. It looked as if he had been in a fight. His face gazed straight up to the night sky. Blood seemed to have come from under his body. The left hand was stretched out, palm upwards.

PC Clark felt perfectly calm, ice calm, and reached for his personal radio to call the police station.

'I've found a dead man,' he reported. 'Can you put me through to the detective on call?'

When the sleepy young voice of the detective came through, John Clark found it was Detective Constable Jester. First Clark explained exactly where he was, and then said, 'Are you coming down, James, or will it be the DCI?'

James Jester was far from calm, he was in a state of excitement.

'I'll have to come and assess the situation, that's the first thing.'

'Right, I'll wait for you here.'

PC Clark whistled a little tune to himself. He'd be here at least ten minutes, if not a quarter of an hour. He made another call on his radio to let his superior know about the delay on patrol. Then he squatted down to have a better look at the man.

Not a drunk—there was no hint of alcohol in the air. Not a tramp—the clothes were casual and old-looking but not like a tramp's. He wasn't touching the body, that wasn't his job, but he noticed red marks on the palm of the left hand. After all, he needed something to occupy his mind during the time of waiting. They were pressure marks, as though the hand had been clutching something firmly and it had dug into the skin. There was nothing there now, the hand was relaxed in death. Nothing on the ground, to have fallen out of the man's grasp.

John Clark's mind was still working clearly, intuitively. He thought about it and decided that the marks would probably fade quickly. They might even be gone by the time DC Jester arrived. He took out his pocket-book and a ball-point and on a blank page carefully drew a diagram of the pattern of red pressure lines. Then he measured the lines with the small pocket rule he used for ruling the pages of the notebook, and marked the measurements on his diagram. He was careful to keep the ruler out of contact with the man's palm. This meant the measurements might not be as accurate as all that but it couldn't be helped. He indicated the position of the fingers in relation to the marks.

When lanky, red-haired James Jester arrived, he was in a nervous state. This was the first time that he'd actually been needed when he was the detective on call, and he was anxious to do the right thing. In the light of a torch he looked around the courtyard at all the impedimenta of the building work that was going on, the scaffolding, the cement mixer, the general apparent disorder of a construction site. It was completely quiet and very dark. The whole area seemed deserted.

He looked fixedly at the body.

'I've spoken to the police doctor,' he told John Clark. 'He's on his way. We have to have him certify death before we can do anything else, but there's no doubt of it, is there?'

'None at all,' agreed PC Clark.

James Jester shuffled about for a minute before saying more.

'It is a suspicious death, I would say,' he

stated.

'Yes. A bit hard to decide much in the dark, but natural deaths don't look like this as a rule.'

There was another pause, and they both wished the doctor would come. The man lying on the ground was about their own age, the sort of young bloke they might well have had a friendly drink with. That made it worse, James Jester felt.

'I'll have to let the DCI know,' Jester said at last.

At that moment the doctor arrived. After making his examination, he too thought it might be classed as a suspicious death. As for the fact of death itself there was, he confirmed, no doubt of it. Jester signed the appropriate forms for him, and the doctor vanished once again into the night.

'I'll go and phone the DCI,' Jester said. 'Is it all right for you to stay here until I get back, John?'

'Whatever happens, you are going to want the area secured, aren't you, and guarded?' prompted John Clark.

'Thanks. Of course, they can be getting on with that.' Jester called the station by radio and arranged for the securing and guarding, then he went off to find a phone. He wasn't used to taking responsibility like this, and his hands were sweaty. How was Acting DCI Smart going to react to being woken up in the middle of the night?

'Mr Smart,' he began when he was connected, 'we have a suspicious death in Coffee Yard. The doctor's been, and I've requested that the area be sealed off and guarded. Do you want to come down and have a look?'

Dave Smart thought that was a funny way to put it, but only said that he thought it would be as well, commended Jester for what he had done so far, and said he'd be down in a few minutes. As he only had to slip his clothes on and travel from his flat in Monkgate Cloisters, it didn't take him long.

It seemed a short time to John Clark and James Jester too, because the uniformed policemen arrived to seal off the area, and various decisions had to be made by Jester in discussion with their sergeant. John Clark went on standing by the body. The silent hours on patrol had vanished into nothing, after all. By the time this lot had finished he'd have to rush round the rest of his beat until he caught up with himself again. Oh heck! He'd have to remember to tell either Jester or Mr Smart about the pressure lines on the hand. If they were still there it wouldn't matter much but if they weren't it might be important.

By the time Dave Smart showed up on the scene, the far end of the alleyway had been sealed off, and the only entrance and exit was now by Coffee Yard into Stonegate.

7

'Good,' said Dave, as a uniformed policeman now on guard in Stonegate noted down his arrival. He wheeled his bicycle into the yard and propped it against a wall. Then he walked over to where James Jester and John Clark were standing. By now Coffee Yard was illuminated by the chancy light of several torches, as well as the sideways light from the lamp on the corner of Thomas Gent's Coffee House.

After a friendly nod to the two younger men, Smart squatted on his heels to look closely at the body.

'Certainly suspicious,' he said quietly when he stood up again, thinking to himself that it was probably murder. 'James!'

'Sir.'

'Tell them to extend the tape round that skip in the road. I want it included in the guarded area.'

James rushed off to see to this.

'I thought it could be murder, sir,' John Clark said diffidently.

'You found him, Jester tells me?'

'Yes, sir. Just after twelve o'clock.'

'You'll be writing out a report, but tell me now.'

At the end of his story, Clark said, 'I happened to notice some marks on his hand, sir—this one, it's his left as you see. It looked as if he'd been holding tight on to something. In case they faded I made a drawing of them.' He

8

produced his pocket-book.

Dave examined the drawing and looked at the man's hand. To be helpful, Clark brought his torch close. Dave peered.

'There's only the faintest indication there now,' he said at last. 'It was good thinking.'

'I was just going to tell DC Jester about it when the security team arrived,' Clark explained.

'James!' Dave called.

'Yes, sir?'

'Got one of those plastic bags for evidence? A biggish one. Oh, thanks. Just the job.' He carefully drew the bag over the dead man's left hand. Then he spoke to the sergeant, who was thinking about leaving and going back to the station.

'I'd like one of those tents that we use for protecting a body,' he said. 'It might rain. Can you have one put up over him? As carefully as possible so as not to disturb any evidence. I've decided to leave the enquiry for a few hours until we have the benefit of natural light.' Turning back to John Clark, he went on, 'You can carry on, constable. I'll be seeing you when you hand your report in. About a quarter past six, say? Right. Good lad.' To James Jester, he said, 'First time you've been called out, James? Well, you didn't do badly. Stay here until they have put the tent up over the body, then you can go home. You're still on call, don't forget. Write me out a report and see I have it before

9

you knock off.'

'You aren't starting the enquiry now, then, sir?'

'We might do more harm than good in the dark. He won't hurt for a short time, then with daylight we'll be able to see what we're doing. Before you go, James, see that there are two uniformed men left on duty, one here in the courtyard and one in Stonegate. We don't want anyone disturbing the tape we've put out there, and there must be someone in here to see that there's no disturbance of the scene.'

* * *

Those were the last words PC Clark caught as he slowly dragged himself away from Coffee Yard and was logged out by his colleague on guard duty. He realized that his taut nerves needed to simmer down. He began to walk briskly on his beat and kept the pace up until he was back on the scheduled time. He had a lot to think about. It was his first experience of anything as dramatic as this. As he glanced at his reflection in a shop window, while trying the shop door to make sure it was fastened, he noticed that his eyes gleamed bright under his helmet.

The moon had come out from behind a cloud and was making the scene around him very lovely, and John Clark was a man who appreciated the charms of an old city centre.

10

He knew enough about architecture and history to enjoy tracing the beginnings of a place from what survived on the ground, to have fun by noticing the pattern of growth and wondering if an older building existed behind a more modern frontage.

This city he lived in had plenty of that kind of interest and no walk through it was ever boring to him. But this beat—well, it had been something else. Something he thought of as real police work.

CHAPTER TWO

Acting Detective Superintendent Robert Southwell was walking—striding—along Stonegate, towards the scene of the murder. Shops built gable-end to the pavement jutted upper floors towards their neighbours across the way, and at the end the great bulk of the cathedral blocked in the view.

Bob Southwell had once said, to his next-door neighbour, that he would never be able to ignore the charm of the city where he had come to work; but now he was taking no notice of his surroundings. He couldn't stop thinking about whether he would be chosen for promotion, and it wasn't until he reached a refuse skip parked in the middle of the very narrow street that his thoughts came back to the matter in hand. The modern skip looked incongruous in its ancient setting. Nothing on four wheels could get past it on either side, and that was how it was going to stay.

Southwell wasn't feeling co-operative that morning. Waiting to hear if he was on the short list for detective superintendent was really getting on his nerves.

The builders weren't going to be too pleased, he thought. The Trust who owned the site and were doing the building work weren't going to be too pleased. Anyone who wanted to go up or down delivering goods was going to be furious. The shop owners were probably going to sue the city council. Tough. 'This is a murder enquiry,' the uniformed man dealing with the public had said a dozen times already that morning when various important people had contacted the police station.

Southwell reached the skip; it was partly outside a shop whose upper floor was supported by a carved devil painted red, and partly outside the alley called Coffee Yard. There was a ribbon of bright plastic defining the area shut off by police, and marking the pathway in through the arched entry, towards the building site where, shortly after midnight, the body of an archaeologist had been discovered.

Acting Detective Chief Inspector David Smart had set up the enquiry, but in the York area the officer in charge of a murder case was normally the detective superintendent. Robert Southwell hadn't been able to come himself until now. Reaching the red devil, he turned behind the skip and into the narrow stone-paved alleyway. As he walked past Thomas Gent's Coffee House and the Nearly New clothes shop, he reviewed the situation he hoped to find at the end, and by now all his faculties were concentrated on the job.

CCTV—Close Circuit Television—were already on their way out, cameras furled, videos taken, tripods folded, waiting politely for him to emerge from the only entrance and exit.

'Got everything necessary?' he asked.

'Sir.'

'See your stuff later, then,' he said and went past them. The officer on duty logged him in and them out.

The builder in charge of the site work, the architect, the director of the Trust, and a few others were standing in a frozen group at the right of the open yard he had now entered. On the left were his own scene of crime officers, ready to start on the next stage in the sequence of enquiry.

On the extreme left, as Bob now stood in the centre of the yard facing the three-storey range, lay the point of the exercise, a man, very obviously dead, flat on his back between a concrete mixer and a dustbin, his left arm lying flung outwards with the fingers flexed as if he had been holding something which he was prepared to defend to the—well, as it had turned out, to the death; but uselessly, for there was nothing in those curved fingers.

Bob Southwell stood close to the body and looked down, then up at the range of scaffolding enclosing mainly empty space except, on the left, the stub of an earlier building. The supposition was that the man had fallen or been pushed from up there, but they wouldn't be sure about anything until the forensic scientist and the pathologist had visited the place, then carried out the autopsy and tests.

The whole building site was quiet as it had not been for months past. No cheery whistles, no distant transistor playing, no sound of hammer or saw. No one present spoke. It was a cold day, but not unduly so for March. The early morning sky visible directly above, between the clustered roofs, was light blue, hardly marred by cloud. The stone paving of the alleyway continued through the yard and out through another archway at the back, but today it was sealed off by the bright plastic tape and a solid uniformed policeman stood there to make sure none of the public or anyone else went in or out that way.

Bob looked down again, and for a while memorized the face and figure which lay before him. Bright blue eyes, gleaming through the almost shut lids. Winter skin, weathered but

14

palish, dark hair under the usual wool cap, moustache and beard, the familiar unshaved, long-haired pattern of young archaeologists. It was a thin face and the body was long but slight, bony, the hands were meagre but looked strong, the cheeks were a little sunken, the skin round the eyes wrinkled, the whole face had a slightly parched look.

It might have been an accidental death, except for the look of fury which seemed to linger on the features, the right hand which was open as if to ward off a blow from in front, the palm scored to the bone by a knife cut, the rips sliced into the clothing, the blood which had flowed out from some unseen wound.

'Right,' Southwell said, turning to the scene of crime team. 'Carry on.'

Normally he would have stayed with them, intently watching, participating. Now, he walked over to the group of onlookers.

'Gentlemen. And ma'am. It is very good of you to wait for me. This is a dreadful thing to have happened. I'm sure you'd like to talk it over. Is there anywhere warmer we can go, and perhaps have a coffee? It's getting sharpish this morning. It seems to be colder now than first thing. Cold enough for snow.'

'The coffee house,' the director said. 'Two of the staff had already arrived before we managed to contact them. They might as well make coffee for us. There won't be any customers as no one is being allowed in.'

The group trailed over and down the alley to the door of the coffee house. Bob Southwell knew it already: the eighteenth-century atmosphere inside, so much more austere than people expected the period to be, the beautifully researched and reproduced fittings, the waitresses in their long print dresses and pretty caps. This morning it had that expectant feeling buildings have before the work of the day begins. One of the two staff who had arrived early appeared and the director went to ask for coffee to be provided.

'Anything to eat?' he asked generally. No one responded.

Bob walked over to the window looking out on to the yard and stood waiting until the others joined him at the table. He could not help contrasting the silent yard with the scene he remembered from a few weeks before.

In the middle of the investigation into a previous murder, the one at the chocolate factory, he had snatched half an hour to be with his family, and they had walked down here to see what progress was being made at Barley Hall. Bob remembered standing for a few minutes to watch. It had been a cold day which had begun with mist and progressed to a sky puffed with grey cloud. A radio had been playing pop music somewhere and one of the carpenters was whistling. The noise of hand-sawing was going on as, bit by bit, the oak framework of the two-storey range went back in place. Bob had been interested to see that the great trees shaped into uprights were being used root end upwards, so that the natural swelling at the bole now acted as a support for inner beams. A hoist rising up and down a ladder made a grating noise. Some men were erecting a small section of scaffold. A pushbike was leaning among the internal scaffolding. Bob remembered that his wife Linda had been fascinated by the tiled roof on top of the two-storey range—it was beautiful with its handmade tiles exactly like the medieval, fin-shaped ridge tiles, and little turret to let out the smoke. One of the waitresses had come into the yard to the dustbins—she had had a mop and bucket and was washing out the waste containers, tipping the used soapy water on the floor. Members of the public had been standing on the flagged path, watching, laughing and talking. It had been a happy scene, not grim, as it was now.

He was roused by the director speaking to him as the others came and sat at the table.

'Coffee won't be a minute.'

The group had been looking curiously at Bob Southwell, not having previously known any high-up policemen. He seemed serious, intelligent, his glasses catching the light and hiding the expression of his eyes. When he had first arrived they had noticed his slender height, his broad forehead, his air of walking lightly on the ground, the faint resemblance he had to the dancer, Fred Astaire. They felt he was not to be trifled with.

Bob turned from the window and looked round at the faces of the group. Their expressions were shocked, as he expected, and worried. It was warmer inside than out in the yard, but everyone seemed cold.

'You must be wanting to ask me a lot of questions,' he said easily. 'Now's your chance. I will have a lot to ask you in return.'

The director spoke first. He spoke quietly, but there was no doubt of his authority and experience; it was in every line of him.

'This is an appalling thing to happen,' he began. 'We're all unspeakably shocked and saddened and don't want to obstruct you in your work. Normally I would close down the site completely, no question about it. Accidents have happened before now, on digs. But this is difficult. There are certain things which affect other people—like the skip in the road...'

'The skip must be properly examined in case it yields any evidence,' Bob said. 'First we want to look at it *in situ*, then it can be taken to the station and kept in case we need it again. As soon as we've cleared that it can go to the dump.'

'It's not the skip going to the dump which is the problem. But we've been very careful to remain on good terms with the townspeople and the traders in Stonegate and this is

18

destroying weeks of effort to keep good relations. George worked more than anyone to keep on the right side of the shopkeepers who are having to work around us.'

Bob paused before he replied. Perhaps he ought to bend a little on this point. There would be other times when he wouldn't be able to be flexible. 'Wait a minute,' he said, and left the table, returned to the yard, and had a word with his second-in-command, Dave Smart, at present Acting DCI, who had just returned to the scene.

'Have we any manpower in the scene of crime team who can do a preliminary on that skip in the road?' he asked. 'See to it if you can, Dave. The natives are getting restless.'

'Surely will, boss,' said Dave.

'We are giving the skip priority,' Bob told the director on his return to the coffee house.

'Thank you. That's good. It will be much appreciated.' He looked down, then with a sudden increase of determination went on, 'There is another thing.'

'Yes?'

'In two days' time we have a crane arriving to lift the big timbers into place for the walls and roof of the three-storey range of the building. We need to prepare for it. We were only just going to be ready in time as things were.'

'Contact the firm and delay it,' Bob replied, but this didn't meet the case, apparently.

19

'You don't understand,' the director said, and a harassed look appeared on his face. 'This is a very special crane.'

The architect spoke. He was a tall, good-looking man and completely wrapped up in the site and its progress. As time went on Bob was to realize that when engaged on a job, the architect's concentration on it was total.

'We spent a lot of time thinking about this matter of raising the timbers,' he began. 'It presents all kinds of special problems on a constricted inner city site like this one, problems which weren't problems when we reconstructed the lower and differently situated two-storey range. A crane is the only practical solution but finding one suited to the site seemed to be impossible. At last we tracked down a crane which could be brought in, used to do the job, then taken out again. It is Italian and has been specially designed to cope with exactly these problems in the centres of their historic cities such as Rome and Florence. Hiring it was hard to arrange and very expensive indeed. Justifying the expenditure and raising the money was extremely difficult. Now, everything is laid on. The crane arrives here very late on Saturday night and is to be parked in St Helen's Square.'

('Not a police matter,' muttered Bob.)

'Early on Sunday morning it's to be brought up Stonegate in pieces small enough to come through that archway from the street. Then it'll

20

be assembled in the yard. The crew to put it up and use it are coming over with the crane—some of them are Italian. There's no way we can alter the arrangements now. The crane is on its way already, it will have left Italy with the men.'

The director broke in. 'If we tell them when they land later today, or early tomorrow, that it's all off, we'll still have to pay and it might be months before we can set up the arrangements again.'

'This is a murder investigation,' began Bob.

'We need two working days to get ready for the crane,' the architect said.

For long seconds no one said anything. It was Thursday morning already.

'Unfortunately murderers don't pick their times with regard to other people's convenience,' Bob went on, quietly. 'I can see what you mean about the crane, but—'

'This whole project,' the architect broke in, 'might be—would be—put in jeopardy. We've worked for years, literally, to interest people and set it up, obtain planning permission and get the job going, raise the finance, find the materials. The building sequence is worked out to the day. I'll fetch you a copy of the time scheme, there's a spare upstairs in the temporary office. Every day's work is planned out, has been planned out for months. We've been fairly fortunate with the weather, but if it had hailed, snowed or flooded, we'd have

21

carried on according to schedule. It had to be like that.'

'Presumably you built in a bit of slack in case there were times you simply couldn't work,' Bob said mildly, wondering how they could have kept to schedule if York centre had been partly flooded and lines of communication cut, which happened often enough to be a consideration in the winter. Then there were the inevitable delays in supplies, which occurred whenever he, Bob Southwell, had had anything at all to do with building anything. A simple little house extension was always held up for supplies which hadn't arrived, and a hundred and one other things. How could a scheme as immensely complicated as he suddenly realized Barley Hall was manage without such delays and problems?

'Any slack that existed has been used. We're nearing the end of the project now. Most of the big crucial jobs are past. Once the roof timbers are in place for the three-storey range, it's steady work of the kind we've had experience with on the two-storey. Then there's finishing off. That sort of work is more adaptable.'

'Look, gentlemen,' Bob sounded firm, 'all I can promise you is that we will leave the site as soon as we possibly can. We would do that in any case. I can't put apprehending a murderer at risk because of a crane, however special and expensive. But I do understand your concern and I'll keep you informed at all times of our progress. You can be sure that we won't be here a minute longer than we need to be.' He thought guiltily of all the times a murder site had been cordoned off for weeks, months, if necessary.

The builder chipped in next. The other members of the group had been sitting absolutely quiet while the director and architect had their say, but Davy Jones could wait no longer. He was a short, square sort of man, growing thin on top, with a wide mouth, and glasses which he was waving about in his hand.

'This is an awful thing to have happened,' he said. 'We've never been held up on a job because of a murder before, and he was a nice young chap. It's really horrible. Makes me feel ill. But my men had to be sent home this morning,' he went on. 'That's wages to pay for no work done. The carpenters and joiners are from another firm on a separate contract— they aren't my concern in that they aren't working for me, but our work fits with theirs, hand in glove. They'll be to pay as well. Every day idle and paid for has to come out of somebody's pocket and it isn't going to be mine.'

'Gentlemen, I do realize that this is a building site, and a very special building site. As far as that goes, we'll be as considerate as we can. Now, suppose you help me with this murder enquiry? You do realize that as soon as we have apprehended the murderer, we will be out of your hair. Most murders are cleared up within two days, right?'

'Most murders are domestic, though, aren't they?' asked an older man who hadn't spoken yet. 'The sort where the murderer goes to the police station and says, "I done her in, guv," or the neighbours tell you the couple were always fighting and they were sure to kill each other one of these days?'

'Or a fight outside a pub,' added someone else.

'You're both right. Most murders are domestic or due to violence when young men have taken drink,' Bob had to admit.

'And some murders take months or years to sort out,' said the girl, who had been sitting silently at the end of the table.

'Let's hope this won't.'

'What can we do to help?' asked the director, his concern for the crane dealt with for the time being.

'As it happens I had met this young man before.' Bob leaned back in his chair, steam from the untouched coffee rising before him. 'A few weeks back my family and I stopped briefly to see how you were all getting on here, and he came up and spoke to us, explaining that he was one of the archaeologists who had been associated with the work and would be pleased to answer any questions. I recognized him at once this morning, but don't know

24

his name.'

'George,' said the girl at the end of the table.

'George Followes,' said the director.

'Can you give me more background?'

'He's one of the Trust's regular staff. He's been with us a couple of years now, and I expect he'd have been moving on soon. They usually want to, though in the present recession they can't often find other positions. He was applying for posts with local authorities—I know because we've had some requests for references.'

'A local man?'

'No. From the north-west, I believe, Cumberland way. Cumbria they call it now.'

'The old county names stick, don't they?' Bob said conversationally.

'The old ties drop away if you move about much,' the director went on. 'We tend to become citizens of the whole country. I doubt if you'll find his background has any significance in this. Young staff find their allegiance to the group more important, and no doubt the tensions within it seem out of proportion at times.'

'You think that's where we should be looking? At tensions within the staff, perhaps those working on site, or between the layers of the hierarchy?'

'I can't advise you. My experience is that every group situation has tensions. I've never known a site free of that, and mostly they're much worse than we've experienced here. Problems due to personal relationships have been very minor.'

'I will need to speak to each one of you individually,' Bob Southwell said. 'Please wait a moment.' He went to the door and called to a young police constable who was standing nearby.

'Officer! Tony Simmons, isn't it? Can you come in here a minute? Got your notebook? Take names and addresses and telephone numbers for me, will you?'

'I must go,' said the director. 'Dr Reiver here will act as liaison—can you do that, Ralph?'

The man who had put in the remark about most murders being domestic nodded. The director, the architect, and Davy Jones the builder gave their details to the constable and left. When the shuffling and footsteps were over, the young constable was gone and the door closed again, quiet settled back and those still round the table sat and looked at one another. Bob felt that the people with the greatest power and influence had left—chief administrator, planner, and practical craftsman.

*   *   *

'Now then,' Bob said comfortably, 'can we get down to brass tacks? You all look as though you had something to tell me. Who's going to be first?'

'I'd better define my position,' said the man called Ralph Reiver. He was considerably older than anyone else in Coffee Yard that day. His sparkling white hair, combed back from a broad forehead, grew to collar length. His face was one which, once seen, was never forgotten. Bob thought he resembled some ancient saint. He was obviously tallish, with an air of gentle humour and bright intelligence; the word which came into Bob's mind to describe him was 'cultured'. He wore a Barbour waxed-cotton jacket over an open-necked shirt and a bright jersey, with cord trousers.

'I used to be on the university staff full-time, but now I'm past retiring age I only work for them a few hours each week. In my own time I'm helping the Yorkshire Archaeological Society with a project of theirs, compiling a gazetteer listing all the ecclesiastical sites, past and present, in Yorkshire. North Yorkshire will be ready first, but we intend to cover the whole county. I've been in touch with the Trust here because these buildings were originally Church property, though it's rather a marginal case for the YAS survey. Being the liaison person between the police and the other bodies involved can come within my scope, in an exceptional situation like this.'

'Right. Do you want to stay now, or ...?'

'Certainly. I can't tell you much personally about George, only having known him

27

slightly, but I'll stay.'

'If you need to be in touch with me any time about this case, this is my telephone number.' Bob passed him a card, then left him out of the questioning.

* * *

The girl who was sitting at the end of the table spoke next, after looking round courteously to make sure she wasn't taking anyone else's turn.

'George and I have been going out together,' she said shyly, then burst into tears. Her dark mop of hair obscured the view of her bent head. She took off her big glasses and laid them on the table, then put a handkerchief up to her face.

The others looked uncomfortable. After listening to her sobs for a short time Bob Southwell said gently, 'Would you like to wait until the end to talk to me? Why not go upstairs to the Ladies and have a quiet few minutes? I can send one of the staff to tell you when the others have gone.'

The girl gave him a grateful look, stumbled to her feet, collected her glasses, jacket and a bulging African basket-type container, and made her way up the staircase towards the upper floors.

* * *

There remained two youngish men.

The first to speak was a different type, pale, almost colourless, so Bob guessed that he was a sedentary worker.

'Marius Caile is my name,' he said, 'as I told the constable. George shared my house and we had some social life in common, but I'm not in the same field at all. I work for the council, in the Guildhall. George didn't talk much about archaeology, though he did sometimes. It all sounded fascinating, more interesting than accounts. If it's all right with you, sir, I ought to get to work. They don't know yet what's kept me.'

'How did you get to know what had happened?'

'I'm told that the police checked with the director early this morning, and he came down straight away.'

'That's right,' agreed Bob.

'The director went to the Trust office and looked up George's details, and rang his home number. I answered and said I'd come down. Before I came I rang his parents and his girlfriend. There isn't much I can do if I go back to the house so I might as well go to work and make arrangements to have some time off. When Mr and Mrs Followes arrive, I need to be free to look after them.'

'We need to examine George Followes' personal possessions as soon as possible,' Bob Southwell said. He rose from the table and went out again into the yard and gave rapid directions to his staff. In seconds one uniformed officer went off in the direction of the Guildhall, and a plain-clothes soco came into the coffee house.

'I have sent a policeman to explain matters at your office,' Southwell said to Marius Caile. 'We need your help for a little longer. Please go with the scene of crime officers and let them into Followes' rooms, will you, Mr Caile? Mr Snowden here is one of the team and will drive you round to your home.'

*   *   *

At last the remaining man, who had not spoken yet, had his turn.

He was more smartly dressed than George Followes had been, and when he introduced himself Bob realized why. Eliot Lleyn was another archaeologist, but was moving from academic work to dealing with the business community. From what he said, it seemed that nowadays most archaeological excavation was carried out on contract to firms who needed to know if historic sites lay under their planned building work. The Trust could tender to do surveys for them and when important remains were found, tender to carry out the careful excavation needed.

He explained this in reply to Bob's questions, and said that the excavation carried out on the Barley Hall site hadn't gone down to the Viking or Roman levels.

'It's a long story,' he said.

'I think I already know some of it—everyone living in York must have heard a lot about Barley Hall. As I recall, this area was one of small workshops of plumbers, joiners, that kind of thing. The alley is a public right of way and often used. There was a good view of the backs of rather decrepit nineteenth-century buildings, cobwebbed windows, doors half off their hinges, gutters about to fall from walls, and so on.'

'It was in danger of demolition. It's natural that you thought the buildings were nineteenth-century; most people did. The Royal Commission for Historical Monuments have given the true picture in one of their books. As it happens, the architect is particularly interested in timber-framed buildings. We used to have many in York— probably most of the city was timber-framed at one time. There were good forests around and plenty of oak. "A wealth of timber," the antiquarians used to say. Plenty of carving and panelling. As fashions changed and the supply of oak decreased, the brick Georgian styles were more popular. Much of the old wood framing was hidden behind brick façades and the old windows replaced by sash ones.'

'The architect knew that what I thought were nineteenth-century buildings were much older?'

'Medieval, with most of the timber framing intact. It excited him tremendously. He'd had a bad experience previously with the old Queen's Hotel.'

'Everyone did, didn't they? I remember how hard the Georgian Society and other interested bodies fought to save the Queen's. Why they didn't succeed, in a town like York, I can't understand.'

'Nor could anyone else,' the young archaeologist said grimly. 'It wasn't only the lovely Georgian rooms and the pleasant façade; our architect discovered that the Georgian work hid an earlier timber structure—three storeys, a very rare survival. The best Georgian room was put in store, and so was some of the other panelling. It was supposed to be reused in the new Queen's—not that anything can compensate—but the timber framework, which could well have been salvaged and re-erected elsewhere—we think that was just smashed down and scrapped. So when he discovered the secret of this area, the architect was extra keen to conserve this.'

'I can see that.'

'Not many archaeologists worked on site, not compared to the Viking digs and so on, because with the intention being to re-erect the existing early structure, there weren't going to be any big new foundations going in, which would have destroyed what lay underneath.

We explored the earlier floor levels, and looked for remnants of medieval building materials, things like that.'

'What was George Followes doing on site, then?'

'He and I kept a watching brief, in turns. We could always talk to the public and put them in the picture if there was nothing else to do.'

'As he did to me and my family, in fact, some weeks ago.'

'Yes. I remember you mentioned it earlier.'

'I never expected to see him again as he is now.'

At this reminder of what it was that lay so silently in the March cold of the courtyard outside the window, the three men round the table were quiet as though holding a minute's silence in George Followes' memory.

'How well did you know George?' asked Bob, breaking the silence.

'As a colleague, another member of a team. We got on OK but didn't seem to be in the same social groups. I only saw him at work.'

'What you've given me is useful background information,' Bob assured him, 'and I'll be seeing you again—there'll be other questions to ask. I still have to have a word with the young lady who went upstairs. It's been a shock to everyone. We might be able to get back to all of you today—if not, probably tomorrow. Let us know where you'll be if not at home or at work.'

'Do you still want me to stay?' asked Ralph Reiver.

'Not really. Is there any work you can be doing here?'

'I could spend some time in the Trust's office, notifying people, that kind of thing.'

'Good.'

In a minute or two the coffee house was empty and Bob asked the waitress if she would mind fetching the girl from the upstairs cloakroom.

The other member of the coffee house staff came from the back regions.

'Is there going to be any chance of us opening for business today?' she asked.

'I doubt it, though my staff would welcome something to drink, and probably eat too, later on.'

'I was thinking we could get on with having a clear-out in the kitchen.'

'Why not? Could you combine that with making a few refreshments?'

'Can do.'

The girl came down the stairs towards them. Her hair had been combed and her face sluiced by the look of it; she was pink from towelling. She was wearing her jacket and carrying a cup and saucer as well as her basket.

'Two more coffees?' asked Bob, with an enquiring glance at the second waitress, who smiled, nodded and retreated into the kitchen. The other one, who came downstairs after the

34

girl, cleared the used pots from the table.

Bob watched the girl walk towards him. He could see that it took courage. Her outsize glasses gave her a vulnerable look, and Bob found the short wavy locks of dark hair appealing, as they fell artlessly on to her forehead and neck. There was something appealing altogether in her round young face with its soft sweet mouth and little straight nose. Young and pretty, yet staunch and brave, Bob decided. It was the combination of the differing qualities which touched the heart.

'Now,' Bob said, 'what have you to tell me?'

'My name', the girl began, 'is Sophie Beans...'

CHAPTER THREE

On the day of the murder it had reached noon. Most of the police force now present at the scene had been up at the crack of dawn, if crack is the word for what had been a creeping, a seeping, of faint light into the night sky over York until the stars paled and disappeared, leaving only the moon, a faint ghost, until it too vanished in the cold brightness of the March morning.

The acting detective superintendent walked over to the acting detective chief inspector, David Smart.

'Dave, coming for a bite to eat?' asked Bob.
'Why not?'

'Back in an hour, Rollo,' Bob said to the detective inspector on site. 'Keep an eye on everything, won't you?'

'Where then, boss?'

'Somewhere we can talk and relax. These city centre pubs are so popular, they tend to be full.'

'Well, it's early. I can think of one where we can be in a corner of the back room and it'll be quiet for a while yet.'

They found themselves shivering as they walked along, and the warmth of the pub was very welcome.

'Heard anything?' asked Dave when they were settled with sandwiches and a pint each. Dave was a thickset, rather red-faced man with crisp black hair. Solid was the word for Dave.

'I won't for a while yet, you know that. How long is it since the super had his second heart attack?' A rhetorical question, but Dave answered.

'It was still January.'

'Then after a while, when they'd decided it must be retirement on medical grounds this time, they advertised the job and gave three weeks for applications.'

'That's right.'

'All over the country, Dave. All over the country. You know the regulations. Every— what—third post or something, they have to throw it open to everyone. If it hadn't been this time—if it hadn't been DS Birch's blessed post—the chances for me would have been a darn sight better.'

'That's right, boss. Surely would. You've had a lot of experience, with the DS being off colour during the last year or two.'

'If he'd been fully fit that work certainly wouldn't have come my way. If I'd had only the competition in our own force to cope with...'

'Odds would have been shorter.'

'Much.'

'Must be nerve-racking,' said Dave comfortably. He didn't mind filling Bob's post while Bob was filling that above him, but he didn't fancy all the hassle of trying for a higher grade, himself. It had been bad enough getting to inspector.

'You don't know who the other applicants are, that's the trouble. Oh well, it won't be long before they decide on the short list. They're doing the paper-sift now.'

'Taking their time about it, aren't they?'

'It occupies about three weeks, I was told. Two have gone so far.'

'Three weeks to sift the applications? They must have had a hell of a lot.'

'They're doing more than putting them into alphabetical order, you know.'

'It's a worry,' said Dave. 'You could have done without a murder at a time like this.'

37

'Oh, I don't know. Takes my mind off it. I might be brooding, otherwise.'

Dave said nothing, but drank his beer. He didn't think his boss was the brooding sort. Still, you never knew with people. He must want to get the job pretty badly. Of course, with a wife and two kids, he would want to get on, win promotion, march forward, make progress ... 'Good sandwiches,' said Dave.

'It's not such a bad thing, having this murder to think about, something more interesting than a domestic. Lucky the Trust had that room vacant above the shop. We've had worse incident rooms by a long chalk. They should have got it up and running by the time we're back.'

'Will have, definitely.' Dave finished his mouthful of bread, beef and mustard, and went on, 'You decided to use HOLMES, then?'

'Yes. This is the kind of enquiry which might lead all over the country. I felt that. Of course, HOLMES is more labour-intensive. Computer work usually seems to be, although that's the excuse they're giving for sacking bank staff at the moment, computers have made them redundant.'

'Always more labour-intensive in my experience. Then the computers are out of date and all the info has to be put on the new ones, and that's a hell of a job in itself.'

'Anyway, HOLMES seemed the best for this one.'

'Good job we've people trained on it.'

'"Be prepared", that's my motto, Dave, like the Scouts. Oh, one thing. Jenny Wren. I noticed she'd come over to work in the incident room on the computers.'

'Yes.' Jenny (christened Gladys) Wren and Dave Smart had become a couple, an item.

'Didn't you say she was thinking of applying for the plain-clothes branch?'

'She was wondering.'

'Since she's over here anyway, I'll take her out when I'm doing interviews. Give her experience and give me the chance to form an opinion about her abilities.'

'She'll be pleased, surely will.'

They only spent half an hour in the pub; the first twenty-four hours of a murder enquiry are the most vital. On the way back the cold seemed to have strengthened to such an extent that Bob and Dave were not surprised to see flakes of snow.

'Bit late in the year for this, isn't it?' remarked Dave, who was a York man and used to mild winters.

'Oh, I don't know.' Bob was from Harrogate and liked the harder winters he had been used to on the higher ground. 'I remember once at the Spring Flower Show—and that's April—it snowed so hard and heavy that the marquees were collapsing all round us and wooden supports were giving way, cracking like gunshots.'

Back in Coffee Yard, the body of the murdered man had long since been removed, as soon as the visit of the forensic scientist and the pathologist was over. Bob Southwell found the head of the scene of crime team and had a word. If the snow went on, their work was going to be hampered.

'Would you like an extra man?' he asked. 'There's a young detective constable who should fit in well. I think you could make good use of him.'

'Who is it?' asked the officer cautiously.

'James Jester.'

'Oh, him.' After a pause, the man said, 'All right, then.'

'I'll see to it,' said Bob. 'You'd better have some polythene and shelter the building, quick. Have you finished outside?'

'Well . . .' and the officer paused again. 'Yes, just about.'

'You're going to have to work as fast as you possibly can. There's a very special crane coming and I've promised them we'll give our best co-operation.'

'Floodlights, then,' the officer said gloomily, 'and overtime. We'd better carry on until last thing.'

Bob Southwell climbed the stairs to see the newly arranged incident room. This was at the front of the building which, on the ground floor, housed the Trust's shop. Above the shop was the incident room. On the floor higher still was the Trust's own office.

Southwell thought the incident room the pleasantest they had ever had, appreciating the seventeenth-century proportions and the panelling, without analysing why the room satisfied him so much. The large later window looked out on to Stonegate itself and the varied buildings there, with tourists and citizens of York passing along, edging round the skip which still took up a central position in the road. It was full of builders' refuse, but as is the way with skips it had received donations during the time it had been standing there and now there was a layer of other waste on top, a worn-out kettle, a good many chocolate and sandwich wrappings, a discarded doormat from one of the shops.

Bob rang the station, and spoke to James Jester's sergeant. 'He was on call all night,' the officer protested. 'He'll be asleep now, I should think.'

'He won't want to miss this chance,' Bob was sure.

'All right, sir. But he's on call tonight as well.'

'I'll ring him myself.'

After waking Jester, Bob Southwell said, 'You've been teased enough, James, about your pocket lens. How would you like to work for a day or two with the lads who use them for

41

real all the time?'

'The scene of crime officers, sir?'

'The very ones.'

'I'd like that.'

'Get over here pronto, then. They've got a rush job on. Don't forget, though, that you're on call tonight. You are probably going to miss a lot of sleep.'

'I can manage, sir.'

Poor lad, thought Bob as he put down the phone. He does get teased. Even I can't resist teasing him. He's going to be a good officer one day, all the same.

As Senior Investigating Officer, Bob Southwell could now start the Policy Book, but before going far with that he needed the first results from his scene of crime officers, then lines of enquiry could be worked out. There had better be a progress meeting.

*   *   *

'Right, lads.' Bob was sitting on the edge of his desk, long legs stuck in front of him, thin keen face at a slight angle, the light reflecting from his glasses so that they could not see his eyes. 'Let's have a quick round-up of where we are so far. Before we start—are there enough of us left on duty outside?'

'Plenty, boss. Inspector Rollo stayed down, and there are a few uniform bods.'

'We haven't had a problem with

identification on this one. His name is George Followes, age twenty-five, an archaeologist working on site, as identified by his employer first thing this morning. I've already seen his work colleague, his flat-mate and his girlfriend, and will be seeing them again shortly. We should soon be getting his fingerprints, I expect, from the forensic scientists. As soon as we do, you can check to see if he has a criminal record, although on the face of it that's unlikely. Some of the lads are at his home now, checking his possessions for possible clues.'

'The rubbish skip's had a first survey, sir. We can move it to the depot and have a better look down there.'

'Organize that, Frank, will you? See it's put under cover. It will need searching for the murder weapon and anything else significant. They are sometimes discarded in very obvious places.' Bob made a note, under 'Lines of Enquiry'. 'So we don't need to check lists of missing persons. His parents are coming later today, I understand. At present there's no need to circulate a description of him, either, or to mess about with dental records.'

'Are we taking it that he and his assailant arrived on foot?' asked a detective constable.

'What about that, you socos?'

'We examined the street carefully as soon as we got here. There were no recent-looking tracks, but it was a fine night and we wouldn't have expected them to show. Older tracks,

43

well, there are so many feet and tyres down any city centre road they blend into one another and it's hopeless.'

'So there was nothing in the open at the front that looked significant or told us how he and the murderer arrived?'

'Nothing, sir.'

Outside the window the snowflakes were whirling now. The men in the incident room couldn't help glancing that way. Anything they had forgotten or neglected that morning during their search of the alley and yard would be likely to be hidden, until the snow melted. At this time of year it must be a freak and wouldn't last more than a day or two at most.

'The same down the back alleyway?' went on Bob.

'The same down the back alleyway, sir. A mass of footprints down the middle, nothing obviously significant at the edges. We looked at the soles of his shoes but couldn't see any trace of them down the alley. In the yard, where the surfaces are different and he'd been yesterday, and around what's going to be a three-storey range of building, we had a careful search but the whole site is dusty and there are hardly any distinct traces of footprints. We assumed that he'd fallen from the third-storey level of the scaffolding, near the top of the stairs which I'm told are eighteenth-century and have been left standing. If I could explain this, sir.'

'You'd better,' said Bob.

'As we look at it from the yard—that's from the south—there's going to be ground-floor rooms and on top a big room going up to the roof. At present all that is scaffolding with, naturally, scaffolding boards for the workmen to stand on wherever they are needed. On the left of that, inside the previous building, was this old staircase, and that is being kept. The outer skin of the building was of a later date and is not being kept; they've demolished it and the scaffolding is there because the new front will be put over that part too. It looks as though the victim and the attacker went up those stairs to the top, where there used to be attic rooms. There are a few part footprints. Possibly a fight broke out there, and they moved outwards to the scaffold boards which run along the front. The victim, driven backwards, seems to have tumbled over the safety rail at the edge of the drop. He was a long-legged man otherwise the rail would have stopped him. That's a working hypothesis.'

'That's how it looked,' agreed Bob. 'So in the open, where snow will be covering up traces right now, you didn't find anything that seemed significant in the yard?'

'No, sir.'

'No useful footprints which might be the assailant's?'

'As I've said, sir, the surfaces are dusty and mostly where footprints do exist they are in a mass. We've made notes, taken photographs, but so far nothing looks significant.'

'We need to do a lot more work to create a profile of the victim. The questions I asked this morning were preliminary, but his colleague said he hadn't seen him at all yesterday, it was the colleague's day off. The girlfriend says he was with her until about 9 p.m. then went back to the house he shared. The flat-mate—or house-mate—said George didn't return, and he—the house-mate—assumed he was staying the night at the girlfriend's. So none of them saw him after nine and so far all their statements are uncorroborated. Our lines of enquiry are fairly straightforward, then. Find what he did after nine at night. Obviously he met the murderer, but was it by chance or arrangement? As you know, if this was a random murder by a person unknown to the victim then that's the hardest to solve, but first we work on the theory that they knew each other. Check the statements and question these people again—I'll do the questioning myself. Discover what his interests were apart from the job and his girlfriend, and his behaviour during the last few days or weeks. Ask around here, find anyone who was awake during the night or who is on night work, question the building workmen. That's enough to be going on with.'

*   *   *

Sophie Beans, finding that she was unable to eat any lunch, had left the university restaurant and walked in the driving snow out of the grounds of King's Manor, across Exhibition Square, and round the corner of the Art Gallery to find herself at the door of the York City Archives. She rang the bell and waited. After a few seconds the door opened and the assistant archivist looked out.

'Oh, Sophie. We were expecting you this morning.'

'Sorry.' It was all she could say.

'You're covered with snow! Shake it off here in the entrance before you come in.'

Climbing the steps and entering the archive office Sophie made her way to the seat she had been occupying the day before. The documents she had been using were lying on the table ready for her. Everything was calm and peaceful. Taking off her jacket, she hung it over the back of her chair and put her African basket on the floor by her feet after extracting her notebook and pencil.

She bent her head over the documents, hoping that she was not going to cry again. One bit of her mind was apart from the rest of her, observing, and telling her that right now she was in a state of shock, it wasn't surprising that she hadn't shed a tear since that outburst in the coffee house, the rest would come soon enough. If only they wouldn't come here—if only she could concentrate on the work for her thesis—she might be able to stay cold and neutral and keep George's death something she didn't believe in, didn't believe had happened, at least until she reached home.

The archivist looked out of her little glass-walled office at the girl with short dark hair and dark-framed spectacles with very large lenses. They were so large that, although Sophie's eyes could be seen at the top of them, most of the space was taken by the upper part of her cheeks, and people talking to her tended to gaze at this pale area rather than have eye contact. Her mouth underneath those lenses was sweet, but today was sadly drooping. Sophie was a short, round person, with a tucked-in strip round her middle suggesting a waist.

Nice girl, thought the archivist. Wonder why she didn't come this morning—as a rule she's too conscientious for her own good, that one.

Sophie found that she couldn't even read the documents she had found so fascinating yesterday. She drew the notebook under her hand and instead began writing in her large, rather unformed script the thoughts the snow had brought into her mind, thoughts which welled up without her bidding, as though that observant other self was dictating them.

'It is Saturday evening,' she wrote, 'and our Yorkist army have arrived near Tadcaster six miles west of York itself. We drew up near a little place called Saxton, and now it is too late and too dark to start to fight. The Lancastrians are close by; tomorrow we meet them, English and Welsh fighting English. There are so many fighting men in the country now since the end of our wars with France, so many men who have been away from home for years and have forgotten any other trade but fighting, so many good archers carrying their war bows, their quivers of arrows swinging at their hips and more in the baggage train. We have never mustered as large an army before, and the Lancastrians the same. But I think this is a battle God will join, for of all things, snow is coming down though it is so late in the year. The reserves have taken shelter where they can in the village, in houses and barns, in tents when they have them, or curled up under the carts, but for most of us, drawn in our battle lines on the open moor between Saxton and Towton, here we stay, sleeping if we can in cold and snow, the wet rusting our steel, the horses unhappy, whinnying for a warm stable.'

'Palm Sunday,' wrote Sophie, 'March 29th, 1461. We woke early, those of us that slept at all, and broke our fast with water and bread before it was light. The snow God sent last night is still with us, blown by the wind. The word has gone along the lines of men, we meet the enemy as soon as the light strengthens, we foot archers in front with the mounted men in their battles behind as usual, grouped to break through and attack when our first arrowstorm

49

is spent. The snow hides everything, men are blurs in the whiteness. The battle cry of the Lancastrians is in our ears already. We stand, peering towards them, we draw our bows and loose the arrows and they fly on the wind with the snowflakes and drive together into the enemy's faces, God with us, their arrows fired into the wind fall short, they land in the ground before our feet. We cry out as if hit and fall back. They cannot see us for the snow blows into their eyes but they loose arrows again and again which fall short again and again while ours fly with wind and snow, strong, killing, sped on their way by God. We shout and scream and roar, and they spend their arrows uselessly until at last they have no more and then—oh then we charge forward and grab up their arrows from where they stick in the sodden earth, and their own arrows are loosed against them and they don't know what is happening, they thought they were killing us, they fall over one another as they run backward and die in heaps and we shoot until all their arrows too have been used against this vast army that that bitch Queen Margaret's Lancastrians have brought against the son of the Duke of York, thinking they can defeat us.

Now we have shot the last of their arrows into them, narrow armour-piercing bodkins or broad war heads. We are on to their lines, clashing together with them, and we throw our bows down and pull out swords and daggers

50

and anything we can find to kill them, the blood lust takes us, as our mounted men come up and look for a way through to fight with theirs. Before we know where we are in the frenzy each side have of killing, the swaying of the fight to and fro across the field of battle, the reserves coming into it as we tire, it soon seems the day is darkening into night again and in our lust and madness we have left the moor covered with dead and the little river is full up with bodies and flows red with our blood and theirs.

The snow has abated and I hear the birds singing as they sang in the early morning, now I remember, for this is their nesting time as it is our fighting time. Then I find my comrade, the one I love best, dead on the ground with his weapons gone and the blood is flowing from his side and his naked hand, cut to the bone, runs blood, everywhere there is blood and again blood, on the snow, which is melting now into the blood, sliding away with it into the good earth . . .'

Sophie raised her head and looked around her as if she did not know where she was. Hastily she packed away her notebook and pencil and put on her jacket.

'I think I'll go home,' she said to the assistant archivist. 'There's something wrong with me. Perhaps I ought to go to bed.'

The older woman looked at her sympathetically.

'You're as white as a sheet,' she said. 'How far have you to go? Do you want a taxi?'

Sophie shook her head. 'It isn't far. I'll be home in ten minutes.'

'Make sure you have something hot to eat or drink or both if you can manage it. You'll be nithered by the time you get back. Shall we book you in for tomorrow?'

Sophie shook her head again. 'I'll ring,' she said. 'I might take a few days off until I feel right again.'

What came over me? she wondered as she put her head down and trudged back to the university flatlet. Writing all that rubbish.

Then her mind went back to the time when she and George had been to Towton. He said that as she was studying the fifteenth century she ought to visit the places and get the feel of them, and Towton moor was not so very changed or different, she would be able to imagine how it was then, when thousands of men—twenty-eight thousand, it was said, though the number was very problematic— had perished in a single day's fighting, and Edward and his Yorkist army had broken the Lancastrians and the cream of the English archers and the flower of English chivalry on both sides lay dead.

It had been a warm summer day but as they crossed the open ground she had felt cold to the bone, the day clouded, and she heard in her ears the clash of steel and confused shouting.

When they stopped walking the feeling and sounds had gone and she asked George if he had felt cold, but he looked at her strangely and said that it was too hot if anything.

That had been the end of it but she had remembered and now the feeling had been back again, much stronger. It was because she identified with the period that she had chosen to study the fifteenth century in the York area for her thesis, but perhaps she was growing too absorbed in it and during this traumatic day she had become not quite herself somehow.

* * *

She had not been back long, when a knock came at her door and it was the detective, the kind, keen-faced one who seemed to be in charge, and another, a woman, tallish with straight medium-brown hair cut short, and hazel eyes.

'DS Southwell and PC Wren,' the tall thin one said. 'May we come in for a minute? I did tell you, Miss Beans, that we would want to question you again today.'

She was looking very vacant, he thought, as though she wasn't all there. In the morning she'd seemed such a bright kind of girl. It was probably the result of shock.

'Come in.' She was opening the door and turning away, clearing a tray which looked as though she had just eaten a bowl of soup.

53

'Would you like some tea?'

Bob reflected that policemen must be offered nearly as much tea as parsons, but said thank you, that would be very nice on such a cold afternoon.

'Is it still snowing?'

'Not as hard. It's just stopping, we think. The sun came out for a minute.'

'It snowed like this in 1461,' she said, 'later in the month, it was the 29th. Now, I wonder, is that old style or new style dating? Had they taken the eleven days into account?'

'I beg your pardon?' asked Bob Southwell.

'It's all right. Talking to myself, really. Have you heard about the battle of Towton?'

'Someone mentioned it the other day. I was in a shop, and the customers were discussing the county cricket team, and the Lancashire side, and the butcher said—did I tell you it was a butcher's shop?—the butcher said, "We beat them at Towton and we'll go on beating them whatever they come for if it's only a game of cricket," and I thought, five hundred years ago and he talks about the battle of Towton as if it was yesterday.'

'The grimmest and bloodiest battle ever fought on English soil, wasn't it?' said Jenny Wren comfortably, as though she was remarking on the size of a sponge cake.

Bob noticed that the girl Sophie Beans seemed to be looking a little brighter than when they arrived. To help her along he

54

decided to tell another story.

'One time when I was being driven to York,' he said, 'we came through Towton which meant nothing to me then. I was enjoying being with my friends and laughing and talking as we approached the place—I wasn't very old at the time—when suddenly a wave of depression hit me out of the blue. Not a thing I'm prone to, either. A few minutes later, as we left the area, it lifted and I felt just as I had before. One of my friends told me that other people have had that experience too.'

Sophie shuddered. In a low voice she told him about her sensations when she had visited the battlefield with George Followes, and how that afternoon instead of getting on with the research for her thesis she had begun to write about Towton as if she had been there. Finding her notebook, she showed him the large, rather frantic script, pages of it.

Bob looked at the end, with the beloved comrade dead, and blood which had flowed from his side, and said gently, 'Don't you think it is this morning's events which have preyed on your mind?'

'Probably,' she answered.

'It wouldn't be surprising.'

'You don't think so?'

The kettle began to sing, and Sophie went over to it and made a pot of tea. When they were all served and sitting round, Bob began to question her again, gently, about her

55

relationship with George Followes.

'We met a year ago,' she said. 'I'd got my master's degree in the summer and decided to go on—they agreed I could. George and I had seen one another around but it was after the degree that we started going to places together. We're both mad about the same period in history and we're—we were—always debating the various questions that people do wonder about. It was a friendship and nothing more, then it developed, like things do, and we began to sleep together. Once or twice we've wondered whether it would become permanent, but we decided not to worry but to let things take their course and see how we felt in a year or two.'

'Very wise,' said Bob Southwell. 'How often did you meet?'

'Most days, really, though odd times we were apart for a week or so, when we went back to see our parents at Christmas, and times when George went to visit a dig. On the whole, though, we've met constantly.'

'You told me this morning that he had seemed different, lately.'

'Yes, he had. It's hard to explain or put my finger on. For the first time I felt that he was keeping something from me, but not anything personal, not like another woman or anything like that.'

'Can you explain a bit more clearly what you felt?'

'I felt that he kept thinking about something he wasn't sharing with me. Not that I minded, because there might be times when I was puzzling over something or planning something and didn't want to go through the palaver of explaining the ins and outs, so didn't say anything to him until it was sorted in my head.'

'And this is the kind of thing you felt George was keeping from you?'

'Yes. An argument with someone at work perhaps. Or a building problem. He said I looked bored when he talked about how Barley Hall was going, but I'm sure I didn't unless he told me the same thing several times.'

'Did he have many disagreements with his colleagues at work?'

'There are bound to be disagreements. George was a bit apt to flare up, but then he'd flare down again, if you see what I mean.'

'He didn't hold grudges?'

'Not really.'

'Sometimes?'

'There were one or two people who got on his nerves, usually because they weren't taking archaeology seriously enough.'

'He was really dedicated—perhaps a bit over-serious about it?'

'Some people thought so.'

'When I met him briefly he seemed a very friendly and pleasant young man.'

'Oh, yes, he was.'

57

'Last night, Sophie—may I call you Sophie? I noticed your colleagues do.'

'Yes, of course.'

'Tell me again about last night.'

'There isn't anything to add to what I told you this morning. We both came here after work. I'd been transcribing some documents at the York City Archives in Exhibition Square and George had been on duty at Barley Hall, keeping a watching brief in case something of archaeological interest cropped up, and chatting to the onlookers at other times, which was ninety-nine per cent of the time.'

'All the excavation is finished, they're re-erecting the building, so it's very unlikely there will be anything new on the archaeology front, I would have thought.'

'You never know, though. Look how they found the helmet on the Coppergate site. The excavations had long finished, the builders were putting in the shopping centre foundations, quite outside and beyond the dig area, a mechanical digger turned something up that looked like metal—and there it was ... Almost unbelievable.'

'So you both came back here?'

'I cooked a meal for both of us, we ate it, we talked, played some music, then he said he was tired and would go early, and he did, about five to nine.'

'What time did you actually finish eating?'

'About...' Sophie hesitated. 'About half-past seven.'

'What did you do after he had gone?'

'Decided to have an early night as well. I like reading in bed and it's more comfortable than sitting in these grotty chairs.'

'What time did you go to sleep?'

'Not till about half-past ten.'

'Didn't wake in the night or anything?'

Sophie grimaced. 'When I'm asleep it takes a fire alarm to wake me.'

'And this morning?'

'I woke about half-past seven and heard the phone ringing on the landing. There's a phone on each landing. It seemed a funny time for anyone to ring. I thought I'd better check it out, and it was George's house-mate to say . . .'

The tears Sophie had been so anxious to hold back decided they could wait no longer. Bob gave Jenny a meaning look and they both rose.

'I'll go, but would you like Constable Wren to stay with you for a while?'

'I'd like to do that, Sophie,' said Jenny.

'It's very kind of you,' Sophie sobbed, 'but I'm longing to be on my own.'

In passing Bob patted Sophie on the shoulder.

'We'll be in touch,' he said, and they left.

Early in the evening Sophie went to bed and sobbed her heart out on her pillow, then went to sleep only to dream of the battlefield of Towton in the gathering dusk of a cold spring day, with a person who was somehow herself searching among the dead and crying out in the pain of loss, looking for one sturdy archer who lay with his face turned to the sky, his features rimed over by snow.

CHAPTER FOUR

By the time that Bob Southwell and Jenny Wren had begun the walk back from Sophie's flatlet towards the incident room in Coffee Yard, the brief fierce snowstorm was almost over. The pavements were covered by soft snow of an appreciable thickness which was rapidly turning to the most unpleasant kind of slush. As they passed a newspaper seller they saw his placard, 'Freak storm, traffic chaos', and they took a gloomy pleasure in talking about what stoppages there would be on the railways and motorways, and how long it would take everyone to reach home that night, as a result of the unseasonable weather.

'Before you go back to the incident room, Jenny,' said Bob, 'what did you think of our little Miss Sophie Beans?'

'Nice girl,' replied Jenny.

'A murderess, do you think?'

'I can't see it. You don't think she did it, do you, sir?'

'Catch the hearts of the jury, wouldn't she?'

'Probably!'

'No, I can't imagine her doing anything violent, but that doesn't mean she didn't. Being asleep alone in your own room is no alibi, Jenny.'

'She seems very disturbed. All those pages of wild writing. I didn't like leaving her alone. Don't you think she ought to see a doctor, sir?'

'I'm going to contact the liaison man— Ralph Reiver—and suggest he does something. He's part of the set-up and will know who in the university to contact. They have a health clinic there, with someone on duty all the time, I think.'

'When did her boyfriend die exactly?'

'We're waiting for the result of the autopsy. I'm going along now. He's probably started. Tell them in the incident room, will you? Oh, and you might give Reiver a ring, ask him if he can either come in or phone me in...' Bob looked at his watch '... let's say a couple of hours. See you later.'

With which Bob branched left along Gillygate towards the York District Hospital, and Jenny walked through the stone archway of Bootham Bar into the inner city. As she turned from Petergate into Stonegate, she saw at once that the rubbish skip had been moved—the middle of the road was empty apart from people walking, and the plastic tape had gone from the area round the entrance to Coffee Yard.

61

When the autopsy was finished Bob and the pathologist went in search of a cup of tea. The pathologist had voted for a beer but they couldn't think of a pub within easy enough reach of the hospital. Neither man felt like walking or driving into York (as they usually did after an autopsy) through the rush hour traffic and the slush which had resulted from the surprise snowfall. There were plenty of tea-bars within the hospital, run by volunteers.

Bob bought a packet of biscuits as well and the pathologist bought a KitKat and a Benn's Bar.

At that time in the late afternoon the voluntary tea-ladies were thinking of packing up and going home early because of the snow, and the waiting area was deserted apart from the two men.

'Just in time,' said the pathologist as he relaxed, flexing his legs while he stirred his plastic beaker of tea and watched the departure of the tea-ladies.

Bob sank his teeth into a biscuit. 'What time did he die, then?' he asked with his mouth full.

'You know it's very difficult to say that. We know he was alive at five to nine and dead by a minute or so after midnight. The police doctor who certified death gives it as his opinion that he'd only been dead a very short while, less than an hour.'

'Can't you tell from the time he finished eating?'

'You know better than that, Bob. Those theories were disproved years ago. I can't possibly tell you exactly when he died.'

'And what did he die of?'

'Want it in a nutshell, don't you?'

'Yes.'

'You were there watching and listening— when you finally turned up, anyway. You know what I was dictating on to tape.'

'Go on, put it in a nutshell for me.'

'There were bruises where one would expect them if he was having a fist fight with another man. I understand the forensic scientists found some scrapings under the fingernails of the right hand which look promising, and they are concentrating too on the area of the left palm. Your people told me that he was gripping something tightly enough in the left hand to leave marks in his skin, still visible when he was found. The pattern of the bruises and other damage is consistent with him having hold of something he didn't want the other man to get, and so only fighting with his right hand.'

'Go on about how he died,' said Bob Southwell.

'At some point in the fight the other man drew a knife and that's when it really got nasty. Until then the bruises are of fists. I would guess that his opponent felt he was losing, or at least not winning, and the knife was a last resort.

63

That's my reading of it. The full interpretation as I see it, and the evidence, will be in the report.'

'The knife must have been Plan B. Followes wasn't a strong-looking man; the assailant probably thought a few thumps would be enough to make him yield whatever it was, if that is what the fight was about.'

'Maybe. Our chap put up his right hand against the knife and was badly cut, might have staggered back but that's guessing again. The other chap took a number of swipes at him, ripping his jacket of denim cloth, and one swipe sank into our chap's side.'

'A death blow?'

'Would have been eventually unless he'd reached hospital PDQ, but he fell backwards, almost certainly as we thought on site, off the scaffolding of what will be the top floor of the three-storey range, tumbling over the safety bar, and down into the yard. The bar's to protect men at work, but no one can legislate for fights and murders. The way he fell, the fall should have killed him irrespective of the knife cut. The pool of blood underneath was from the wound. Blood went on flowing for some minutes at least.'

'You mean he didn't die for a few minutes?'

'No, I don't mean that necessarily. Blood stops spurting from arteries at death but there is still an appreciable trickle from cut vessels. He could have died immediately, or else within a very short time.'

'He wouldn't be conscious, though,' assumed Bob, grimacing at the thought of the fall, and the body between the concrete mixer and the dustbin.

'No. Not conscious.'

'My next job is to go to see his parents—they're arriving soon from Cumbria.'

'Rather you than me.'

'It might be easier if they know he wasn't conscious at the end.'

'He wouldn't know anything once he hit the ground.'

They drank what was left of their tea.

'I could have done with another cup. Better still, I could have done with a beer. Or two beers,' said the pathologist, looking at the closed tea-bar.

*　　　*　　　*

On the phone, Ralph Reiver agreed to take on the care of the girl Sophie Beans, and said he'd go round first thing in the morning. There didn't seem to be any reason for thinking she'd do anything foolish between now and then. He was relieved to hear that the skip was gone and said he'd let the director know, and then enquired whether they'd be able to carry on with the building work the next day.

Bob hesitated before replying to this. The timing of the snowfall was unfortunate, but his scene of crime officers had told him that most of their outside work had already been done. They had more work to do, but if the three-storey site was sectioned off they didn't see why work shouldn't go on over the rest of the area. So far there was no sign of the murder weapon. No doubt the murderer had carried it off with him, but they hadn't given up looking.

So with a slight feeling of apprehension that he might be doing the wrong thing, Bob said work could be resumed in a limited way in the morning, and possibly fully after midday. At least, he thought to himself, the workmen will be here, and that will make it easier to question them.

Reiver rang off, absolutely delighted, and, fulfilling his task as liaison person, let the director and the firm of Jones and Jones know immediately. Davy Jones said he would notify the firm of woodworkers, and the director called a meeting of those most concerned, to discuss the position *vis-à-vis* the crane, which was due to reach the dock in Southampton that night, and be unloaded first thing next morning.

*　　*　　*

Meals went by the board when there was a murder enquiry. Bob's wife Linda was not surprised when she heard an apologetic husband on the phone, saying he didn't know when, and she answered in a resigned tone that she had put a casserole in the oven and he needn't worry, she'd turn the heat off now it was cooked and heat it again when he did manage to stagger home.

'I hope you didn't drink too much with that pathologist,' she added with a slight edge to her tone.

'I don't know what you mean.' Bob did his best to sound shocked and affronted. 'We had a cup of tea.'

'That's a change.'

'And I only had one beer at lunchtime with Dave.'

'I might have known there'd be more to it than a cup of tea.'

'Since when did you object to the amount I drink, which isn't much, I might add?'

Linda stood there looking at the phone and feeling herself softening. Her backbone was reinforced by the conviction that the more fuss she made the more effort Bob would make to get home in reasonable time, say before twelve midnight, and make another effort to eat a meal. She knew only too well what would happen otherwise: he'd stay on the job until all hours, worrying away at the problems, and in a few days he'd be worn to a frazzle and as bad-tempered as hell.

'See you later then—not too much later,' she finally said, and put the phone down. Bob at the other end felt slightly mystified. Was she annoyed, or wasn't she? He thought he'd try to be home reasonably early in order to find out. Meanwhile, he had to see George Followes' parents, and he'd promised himself to see George Followes' flat-mate, and Eliot Lleyn, the second of the duty archaeologists, before knocking off tonight; he'd better get on with it.

'The media have been on at us all afternoon,' remarked Jenny Wren, who was working on a nearby computer, when she saw him putting on his coat.

'We had a press conference this morning,' Bob objected. 'They shouldn't have pestered after that. What have you been saying to them?'

'I haven't been saying anything. The Press Office have been dealing with it.'

'If anyone else from the media contacts us,' and Bob was speaking to everyone in the room, 'tell them 11 a.m. tomorrow for a press conference. Fob them off till then, right?

'I've two more interviews to do, and see the poor chap's parents,' Bob went on to Jenny as he buttoned his coat. 'Then I'm going home, or else there might be a domestic crisis. You're intending working late, I take it.'

'The computer entries to finish, sir. Sandra here is taking over for the night shift.'

'Good. You've just arrived, Sandra? Jenny, I'd like you to come with me. Sandra, can you finish the computer entries, and tell your sergeant, when she comes back, that Jenny and

I are going first to Followes' flat, or house or whatever it is, then to see Mr and Mrs Followes, then to Eliot Lleyn's, he has a house near the university, then we will both knock off and go home. I'll call in then in case there's anything I need to know, otherwise I'll be in first thing in the morning and we'll start as usual with a briefing. Right?'

'Right, sir.'

'Goodnight, everybody,' Bob said generally to the handful of constables doing the clerical work on the case.

*　　*　　*

The home George Followes had shared with Marius Caile turned out to be a street house in the Groves area, just outside the city walls to the east. This was an area of small houses, pleasant in its general atmosphere, with a few slightly larger houses, some with early nineteenth-century charm; other houses had been demolished and their place taken by blocks of flats, both private and corporation. There was a church, St Thomas's, a school or two, a few workshops here and there, and a splendid view of the Minster. The fierce through traffic avoiding the city centre had been calmed by a system of one-way streets, sleeping policemen, chicanes and bollards.

The door was opened almost immediately Bob Southwell knocked on it, by the pale youth he remembered from the morning.

'Come in.'

There was a narrow passageway, with a door on the left and one straight ahead.

'That was George's room.' Marius gestured to the door on the left. He led the way ahead, past the steep stairs, through to a living-room with dining-table and four chairs, and two small fireside chairs in front of a gas fire. In front again was the door to a small kitchen.

'Would you like to sit down here? Is this all right?'

'Fine.' Bob took a dining-chair instead of the fireside chair Marius would obviously have preferred him to choose, and waved to Jenny to sit in one of the others. 'What's upstairs?'

'My two rooms and the bathroom.'

'So how did the sharing work in practice?'

'Actually I'm buying the house, but it's a big strain on my salary so I advertised for someone to share. George has been with me for a couple of years now, we always get—got—on really well. I suppose I have the best of it, two rooms to myself upstairs, but after all it's my house, and George was quite happy. The front room is a bed-sit, it's entirely his.'

'We've already searched his room, of course,' Bob said. 'Did the team go over the rest of the house?'

'No.'

'Perhaps it would be as well if you let them do that.'

'If you think it's necessary,' Marius said rather stiffly.

Bob only smiled, so Marius went on about George and his bed-sitting-room.

'He said he could work well there. This room we shared, in that we often cooked and ate together, always breakfast and often the evening meal. Almost always the evening meal until George started going out with Sophie.'

'Have you a girlfriend, then, Mr Caile?'

'Not at the moment. I have a pen-friend. We've met and liked each other very much—we spend holidays together. She's Canadian. I've exams to take, I'm hoping to be a chartered accountant eventually. I'd like to wait until then before getting married.'

'Sounds good.'

Bob could guess that Marius was a quiet inhibited sort of chap, and the pen-friend romance would suit him. Remembering that in the morning he had thought Marius looked like a root vegetable, he thought so even more now. A parsnip, he decided. The pale bumpy forehead and the tapering away to chin level, the light-coloured clothing topped by a Fair Isle pullover, the air of rarely exercising in the fresh air. He had better listen, Marius was still talking.

'We shared the kitchen and bathroom. This room was George's whenever we weren't both using it.'

'Let's talk about last night.'

71

'George said at breakfast that he was going to Sophie's for the evening meal. I saw him for a few minutes because he was here, washing and changing, when I arrived back from work. About ten minutes later he said, "See you," and went. He always said that, "See you." I made myself a meal, ate it, washed up, then went out to the pub. The night before was night-school and I felt like some time off. The Brigadier is over the road, at the end of Monkgate, some of my friends go there. I went to bed at about eleven. George wasn't back, I thought he'd probably decided to stay the night at Sophie's. He had a key, if he should return later. I was woken this morning by the phone—the Trust's director ringing me to say what had happened. I rang Sophie straight away. You know what I've been doing since then. Tonight was night-school again, but with having George's parents to think about I didn't go.'

'I was planning on meeting them tonight.'

'They're at a guest house. There's a card here somewhere.' Marius found the guest house's card on the mantelpiece and handed it to Bob. 'They're pretty shattered, actually. Could you leave it till morning?'

'It had better be tonight—only briefly, though.'

'They could have stayed here but they didn't want to.'

'Better on their own, I'm sure. Have you

72

been into George's room since he was last here?'

'Only for his telephone book. Usually he left it next to the phone...' Marius indicated the wall facing the kitchen, which had a small table, with telephone, against it '... but he'd taken it into his room for some reason. I went in, got it, came out again.'

'No one else has been here as far as you know?'

'No. His parents didn't want to. I took them to a café for a snack and pot of tea and then to the guest house. They looked shattered, worn out.'

'Our men might want to go through his room again. And if we are checking through the rest of the house, they'd better come back tomorrow. Followes' parents will be in touch with you about his things.'

'Of course. Your men have all the keys, and a Yale for the street door.'

'Now. Tell me about him. What he was like. Cross in the mornings? Fussy about what he ate? Anything. The lot.'

'University, you know. Better educated than me, but not earning much, although I'm not, either. George wasn't interested in money. He talked about money-grubbing, that was his attitude. The expression "on the make" was absolute condemnation of somebody. If you heard him use those words, you knew they'd had it.'

'Had it in what sense?'

'He wouldn't want anything else to do with them.'

'I see. Go on.'

'No, he wasn't grumpy in the mornings. Quiet, but not bad-tempered. Never was bad-tempered. He could flare up sometimes, but it didn't last.'

'That's what Sophie said.'

'She's right. We had the odd bust-up, but nothing to mention. We've settled down, I suppose. The arguments were mostly at the beginning, before we got used to one another. George was a quiet chap, did a lot of working at home. He has a computer in there. Read a lot. Keen on Film, you know, with a capital F, Cinema. Old black and white films, classics, good new ones as well, they show them at the university and at City Screen. He liked a glass of wine, but didn't care much for the ordinary pubs. His friends were mostly from the university or the Trust, whereas I was born in York, you see—I have old school friends, that kind of thing. I went out a lot more than he did, until Sophie.'

'He didn't have lots of girlfriends, then?'

'Friends, but not girlfriends. Might have done before I met him.'

*　　*　　*

Bob stopped in the street outside, underneath a street lamp, and reached out a hand to Jenny.

'Let me see your notebook,' he asked. She handed it to him and he flipped the pages. 'Good,' he said then, and handed it back. As they walked on, Jenny wished he had been more forthcoming. Only saying 'Good' was rather unnerving, she felt.

They went next to the guest house where Mr and Mrs Followes had been deposited by Marius Caile, and interviewed them in the general residents' lounge, which was empty at the time. It was an incredibly difficult moment in anyone's life to be interviewed and a stilted place in which to do it. Every action and sentence seemed to be artificial in the circumstances, but Bob did his best. It wasn't the first time such a task had fallen to him. Jenny looked generally sympathetic and sat quietly in the background.

After Bob had greeted Mr and Mrs Followes with much longer handshakes than he would usually have given, they all sat down and looked at one another.

Mr Followes was tall and dark like his son, but a rubicund, chubby man. George's pale complexion, thin build and intense expression had obviously been inherited from his mother. They were wearing formal clothes; Bob thought they would have been happier in more casual outfits, but had felt that to come looking as they did was necessary to show their respect and love for their son. He thought that was probably how he would have reacted himself.

'You already know what has happened,' he said gently. 'It must have been a great shock to you both. I'm in charge of the investigation and wanted to see you and reassure you that you can come direct to me for any information or help I can give. We've been looking into the circumstances of your son's death since first thing this morning and of course, the investigation has a long way to go yet. Is there anything I can tell you now?'

'Can we see him?' asked George's mother.

'I should think so. I'll arrange that for tomorrow morning, if that will be all right, and send round a policewoman to take you and look after you.'

'Can you tell us how he died? Could it have been an accident?' asked Mr Followes.

'There would have been the possibility of an accident, as he fell from the third-storey level of what will be the higher range of building, if he had not obviously been engaged in a fight prior to that. The other person had a knife, and I'm afraid that George had been wounded.'

Both parents looked at him with faces wiped clean of emotion.

They are in shock, Bob thought.

'The fall rendered him unconscious,' he pressed on. 'He would have been unconscious until he died, and would not have been aware of pain. The whole fight, and the fall, probably only took up a very short time. Until that he was living a perfectly normal, happy life, as far as I can tell. Had he given you any indication that something was worrying him? Any change in him at all that you can think of?'

'He said nothing in his letters or phone calls about anything,' Mr Followes answered.

'We liked his girlfriend,' Mrs Followes said.

'Yes, Sophie does seem a pleasant girl. She's very distressed, of course. He had eaten his evening meal at her flatlet and left there about nine o'clock last night. Perhaps you would like to see her tomorrow? It might be helpful to both of you.'

'We'll ring her first,' said Mr Followes.

'Good idea.'

A silence fell.

'When can we take him home?'

The question Bob had been dreading.

'Not immediately, I'm afraid. Not until after the inquest. Then it depends on the coroner's verdict, and on our researches, how soon you can have his body.'

'There was something worrying him,' Mr Followes suddenly volunteered. 'Had been for a few weeks. He wouldn't come straight out with it to us, there was nothing you could pin down, nothing really to tell you, as we just said—but we knew.'

'I'm sure you're right. Other people have mentioned that to me. What a pity he didn't tell you what was the matter. You can't guess at what it was?'

They shook their heads.

'How long are you staying?'

The two parents looked at one another.

'That's hard to say,' the father said at last.

'If I may, I would like to talk to you both about George before you go home, but I don't want to distress you, particularly not now.'

'We want to help, in any way we can.'

'I'll call round tomorrow after you've been to see him, and if you both feel up to it, we could talk then.'

This was agreed, and with more long handshakes they parted.

As they left the guest house, Bob wondered whether to fetch his car from the police station or to take a bus, or walk to Heslington. Then he worked out the mileage, plus the mileage home again, and decided that walking would take too long; he wasn't sure where to catch the bus, and besides, there was all the slush to contend with. Jenny wouldn't be too keen on ruining her shoes.

'We'll go to the station and pick my car up,' he informed her. The walk to Heslington would have been welcome. Even in the messy state of the roads and footpaths, he knew that the physical exercise would have refreshed him and driven the megrims out of his head.

*　　　*　　　*

Heslington is a village which lies east of the city of York. Originally it had a large and splendid

78

manor house, Heslington Hall, and a nucleus of farmhouses and cottages, with church, pub and post office. Then during the 1939–45 war the manor house was taken over by the air force to be used as the basis of command. The owners had moved out to a farmhouse they owned in the village, made the farmhouse more suitable to themselves, and created there a large and lovely garden.

Later, when the foundation of a university in the ancient county town was mooted, Heslington Hall and its grounds, now empty, suggested itself as a suitable spot for the creation of a campus. Daringly and imaginatively designed round a large newly created ornamental lake, modern colleges and concert halls, libraries and laboratories rose up on the rolling pastoral slopes at the back of the old Hall, which was also pressed into use.

With the university came staff and students and the general population who are attracted to the vicinity of a university; new housing went up on the outskirts of the village; older houses were bought and transformed.

To this modern Heslington Bob Southwell drove on the March evening which, with the snowy slush, was giving a good imitation of December, except that it was a good deal lighter. He approached the village from the direction of the Hull road, branching off down Field Lane for a mile or so, a scatter of new houses on his right, before reaching the church and the old village. Having already consulted a map before starting, he drove through the village without stopping until he reached a few new roads on the other side, lined with small newish houses, many of them linked together into a series of bays. The architecture was novel and he looked around with interest. Small trees and large shrubs were well established, now with a picturesque layer of melting snow to give them extra interest.

It was not easy to see the numbers on the houses but he soon identified the one which belonged to Eliot Lleyn.

'Do you know this area?' he asked Jenny as he parked the car.

'Not really.' She followed him up the path and waited as he knocked at the door.

Eliot Lleyn admitted them through a tiny lobby to a through sitting-room, not very large, furnished tastefully with curtains of natural linen, a carpet matching in colour, renovated second-hand furniture, book-shelves, some architectural prints on the walls, and a few colourful and interesting dhurries strewn about. There was another man there, sitting at ease on one of the two sofas.

'Jack Henniker, my co-owner,' Eliot said.

The co-owner was taller than Eliot and his dark hair was fastened back in a pony-tail. He had an air of negligent distinction. Instead of rising to greet the newcomers, he waved a hand at them, a casualness Bob did not care for.

'Jack knew George,' Eliot explained. 'We were all students together. Jack did architecture. You can talk with Jack here. He knows all about it.'

'We don't want to spend too long tonight,' Bob said, partly because he was remembering Linda's voice on the phone. 'Tell me about George.'

Jack Henniker began to chew gum with an air of disinterest, letting Eliot hold the floor.

'We went through university together,' he said.

'Which university?'

'This one.' Eliot looked surprised at the thought of there being other universities in the world. 'We were never close, to be honest,' he went on. 'I've seen more of him since we've both worked for the Trust. We were on the team doing the recording as the old buildings were taken down. Every piece of timber framework had to be carefully recorded, whatever condition it was in, and retained. We were both involved in excavating down to the medieval floor level—I don't know if you've seen it but we uncovered a section of the matrix of a tiled medieval floor. The impression of the tiles was shown exactly, but there were only a few fragments of the actual tiles surviving. They've reproduced them and they're going to put them down soon. Since that part of the work was over, both George and I have been on this watching brief cum public relations job at Barley Hall. That didn't mean we saw much of one another, because we worked alternately, and when not on duty there was plenty to do back at Trust headquarters in Pavement.'

'Something tells me you didn't like him much,' Bob said.

Eliot shrugged. 'He was all right.'

'Bit of a wimp,' put in Jack. 'Always going on about ethics.'

'Should have had a soapbox,' added Eliot.

'Now if you'll give me a run-down of your movements last night from nine o'clock on, we'll be going and leaving you in peace.'

'Why do you want that?' Eliot sounded truculent.

'Only for purposes of elimination. We will be checking on all his friends and colleagues, everyone who knew him, as far as we can. Normal procedure.'

'We'd been to an auction sale during the day, bought a few bits and pieces, arrived back here for a meal, then went out in the evening to the pub in the village.'

'That's fine, Mr Lleyn. Now can you tell me the names of anyone who can confirm that for us?'

They thought of a few people and Jenny wrote the names and particulars down.

'We'll almost certainly think of more queries we would like your help with, so let us know if you are going out of town for any reason, will

82

you?' Bob said agreeably at last.

As they reached the car Bob asked Jenny where her own car was, and if she would like a lift. She explained that her car was in the Lord Mayor's Walk car-park, and he ran her there. As she was loosening her seat belt he said, 'What did you make of that little lot?'

'The two men we saw last?'

'Everyone.'

'Marius Caile is a funny one. Not that easy to live with, I shouldn't think.'

'No. A very odd bod.'

'I was terribly sorry for Mr and Mrs Followes. They were being very brave.'

'People are brave. Ordinary people, when meeting a crisis in their lives.'

'Then the two at Heslington...' Jenny wondered how to put her feelings into words.

'Yes?'

'They didn't tell you much about George, did they? Loads of background information, but nothing on the personal side.'

'That was the case this morning, too.'

'Odd, when they'd known him for years.'

*　　　*　　　*

Bob turned up Ouse Avenue at a reasonable time considering it was the first day of a murder enquiry, and as he went into his house caught Linda's quick upward smiling glance from where she knelt by the cooker. She was in clean jeans and a white jumper.

'Just right,' she greeted him. 'It's hot and not spoiled.'

Bob suddenly realized that he was famished. The worries of the day dropped from him. For once he was going to be able to forget the case, he thought.

'I'll just wash and change, love,' he said. 'These sort of things make you feel grubby all over.'

'Two minutes,' she warned him.

The idea of worries falling away did not become reality. No sooner was he seated in front of a piled plateful of delicious food than Linda said, 'Any news of the short list, darling?'

All the tension of trying to obtain a post at a higher level came flooding back.

'You know we can't expect it before next week.'

'They take a long time, sorting out a few names, don't they?'

'That's what Dave said to me today. I wish you would all shut up about it.'

'No payment for overtime,' sighed Linda, looking at the clock.

'If I get promotion overtime would be a thing of the past. Even if a super works all the hours God sends he only has his salary. Don't forget it's a good bit bigger.'

'Of course.'

CHAPTER FIVE

At the briefing the following morning, after his introductory remarks, Bob went on, 'We will start today on creating a profile of the victim. It will take more work to decide on elimination criteria for his assailant. Obviously anyone who can be proved to have been elsewhere at the relevant time will be out of it. We need more work on tracing the victim's movements between 9 p.m. and midnight. Colleague, girlfriend, and house-mate all say they didn't see him during that period.

'They could, one or all of them, be lying!' Bob spoke the last sentence out loudly, and everyone jumped and paid extra attention.

After a short silence Bob continued.

'So far all their statements are uncorroborated, except that of his colleague, who spent the evening with the co-owner of his house, at the pub. They say they went straight home after the pubs shut. I want independent evidence on that.'

Again he paused, and then turned to the white plastic-surfaced sheet in front of the group, on which he was writing his headings.

'Our lines of enquiry are fairly straightforward. Obviously he met the murderer, but was it by chance or arrangement? We need to eliminate these four people—I'm including the colleague's friend who supplied his alibi—from suspicion and check their statements, by finding other witnesses. I'd like you to ask their neighbours if they observed anything unusual, anyone entering or leaving the buildings where these people live. A questionnaire has been made out for you to use. You could show neighbours a photograph of the victim, but also enquire after other people.'

He went on writing the fields of enquiry to be tackled, on the white sheet.

'So who did he know? It seems most of his friends would be connected either with the university or with the reconstruction of Barley Hall. We can't tackle every student in the university, but you can have a message circulated asking whoever knew George, even if only slightly, to contact us, and you can interview the lecturing staff who teach archaeology students. The workmen here on site are not as numerous, we can interview all of them, their wives or girlfriends, and the bosses.

'A scene of crime team checked out his bed-sit yesterday. No clues to the murder. I suggest we check out the rest of the house today for possible evidence. Mr Caile has agreed to that, so today, lads. He is buying the house, rented George the front downstairs room as a bed-sit and shared with him the dining-room, kitchen and bathroom.

'We need to discover more about his behaviour during the last few days or weeks. The victim's parents sensed something was the matter. His girlfriend also testifies that something was wrong. If we can find out what was bothering him we may have the key to the whole thing.

'Ask at all the properties around the site here, find anyone who was awake during the night and ask them if they heard or saw anything between 9 p.m. and midnight.

'The team who were working on the scene of the murder yesterday—I'll come with you as soon as we've finished here and we'll decide when we can allow the builders full access again. They've this special crane coming from Italy and if we can let them proceed with that work I think we should do so.'

*   *   *

At the same time as Bob was holding his briefing, Ralph Reiver was knocking at the door of Sophie Beans' flatlet. She opened the door still pushing one arm into its sleeve, her hair tangled round her head, and no glasses on.

'Oh, Dr Reiver!'

'How are you this morning, Sophie?'

'All right, I suppose.'

He could see by her swollen eyes and the soft tremble of her lip that she was struggling to keep herself from crying.

'May I come in?'

'It's all in a mess,' said Sophie, but she opened the door and moved a jumper from a chair so that he could sit down.

'I promised that tall thin policeman I'd keep an eye on you,' Ralph said humorously.

She summoned up a laugh, then said, 'That was nice of you. It was nice of him, too.'

'You don't want to take time off from your studies and go home for a few weeks, Sophie?'

She shook her head. 'I'm better here, I think. No point in making other people miserable as well. The best thing would be if I could forget myself in my work, but that idea wasn't too successful yesterday.'

'Oh?'

'No. I went to the City Archives and instead of doing my notes I found myself scribbling the most awful rubbish.'

'Really? May I see?'

'It's quite scatty,' said Sophie, but she fished her notebook out of the African basket and passed it to him. 'I'll go and do my hair, if you'll excuse me.'

When she came back he had finished reading. The notebook was lying on the table and he was leaning back with his legs crossed, gazing into space.

'Coffee?' she asked.

'Please. Let me tell you something, Sophie.' He rose and stood looking out of the window, all the time talking with his head turned away

88

from her. 'It happens that two friends of mine who have experienced bereavements both reacted by writing. This gave them a safety valve, I suppose. They both wrote reminiscences of their lives, and it seemed to help them come to terms with things. You are studying York in the medieval period and that was George's favourite time, too. It doesn't seem at all strange to me that you reacted in this way. In fact I suggest that you go on with it.'

'Go on writing as if I was there?'

'Yes. Why not? You might make something of it in the end. It would stimulate your imagination and certainly not be wasted.'

'You mean don't worry if I can't do my normal work, but let this come out instead?'

'That is exactly what I mean.'

The coffee was made by this time and Sophie put a tray on the table with the cafetière, brown sugar, milk, and two cups and saucers. 'I'm sorry I haven't any biscuits,' she said.

At that moment the phone rang on the landing and she went out to answer it, saying as she went, 'Please help yourself to coffee.'

After a while she came back, poured a coffee for herself and told Reiver that the call had been from George Followes' parents.

'They're going to see George this morning and Mr Southwell, that tall thin detective, is questioning them again this afternoon, so they've asked me to go over about four o'clock.'

'Have you met them before?'

'One weekend. George took me. I think we all liked one another.'

'About your writing ... I don't altogether agree with you over the battle of Towton. Tell me ... are you Welsh by any chance?'

'My mother is,' answered a surprised Sophie, 'but what has that to do with anything?'

'Only that—as you will remember—Edward was the Earl of March; when his father was slain at Wakefield by Queen Margaret's forces at the end of December 1460 he raised, so it is said, ten (some say thirty) thousand fighting men from the Welsh borders, and went to London where he established his base, while King Henry VI and the queen fell back on York. After Edward was made king in London at the beginning of March he went north to fight their forces, presumably with his thousands of border Welshmen, plus thousands from southern England, probably mainly Kent. Meanwhile Queen Margaret had been recruiting extra men from the north, including hundreds, perhaps a thousand, from York itself. The battle of Towton was a defeat of the north by the south.'

'The Welsh archers were famous,' murmured Sophie.

'In your imaginative reconstruction, you take the side of the largely Welsh army, which is why I asked if you were Welsh. In York, the queen had been much the most active partner in organizing their forces against Edward's, while Henry VI spent his time praying. No doubt when, after winning the battle so decisively, Edward advanced as the king and queen fled northward, his victorious Welsh and southern English army would have shown little kindness to the city of York. If you remember, Edward sacked a manor house at Fulford because it belonged to one of the queen's adherents. They say York's hatred of him began with Towton.'

'All those Yorkshiremen slaughtered by his Welsh and Kentish archers? But it was natural that Edward wouldn't feel much kindness for the city either, would he, when he approached Micklegate Bar and saw his own father's and brother's heads stuck up there on pikes ... imagine ... and that paper and straw crown they'd put on his father's head...'

'Don't imagine that bit, Sophie. It will distress you even more. I'm only suggesting that with your Welsh ancestry, you instinctively took up the side of the Welshmen.'

'Shakespeare said, "York will overlook the town of York"...'

'But he didn't overlook it, did he? Shakespeare could never have been here, or else he couldn't resist using the phrase.'

'The heads looked out from the city walls, not inward.'

'That's right. But he might have used "overlook" in the sense of guard, superintend, do you think?'

'Do you realize, Dr Reiver, you've turned the accepted notion on its head? People talk of the Yorkist army defeating the Lancastrians, but it was a Yorkist army of Welsh and southern English defeating a Lancastrian army containing mainly men from the city of York and the rest of the north.'

'All the northern aristocracy and their men were fighting for Henry VI, their anointed king—Percys, Cliffords, Rooses and Dacres. History is rarely the way people believe it is.'

'York really was important in those days, wasn't it? My impression from the records is that it was second only to London.'

'I'm sure that's right. We weren't as independent as London, though. London could almost play the role of king-maker. In the end York always put its trading interests first, before other loyalties, you'll notice that again and again. But it seems to me that the hearts of the people of York were touched by King Henry VI's prayers, and his pious life, poor sod. That, and losing so many local men at Towton, set them against Edward's claim to the throne. They had no choice but to let him into the city after he had won the battle, but you notice some years later, when Edward returned from exile, they wouldn't let him in until he said he had come to support Henry VI, and made all his men shout out "Henry!"'

'He did a Mark Antony, that time,' said Sophie.

'Only he was saying, "We come to praise Caesar, not to bury him."'

Sophie would not have believed, when she opened the door to Dr Reiver that morning, that she would be having a conversation on history with him within an hour, as calmly and sensibly as this.

When Ralph Reiver had finished his coffee he stood up and said he must go; no, thanks, he wouldn't have another one.

'Take care now, Sophie. Make sure you eat and look after yourself. Carry on with your writing. Give me a ring if you feel like talking. If I don't see you before, I'll call round on Sunday, the day after tomorrow.'

* * *

Ralph Reiver was a tall man, who bent his head forward a little as he moved, and so seemed less tall, more hesitant. He was a scholar, an academic. As he walked back into town he thought of how the past influences the present, particularly if you are a student of history and living in York. He expected Sophie Beans could visualize exactly how the city had been all that time ago.

Then he began to think about the medieval timber frame which had been found and carefully taken to pieces when the old buildings on the Barley Hall site had been demolished. Those very beams of wood were to be put back again soon with the aid of the Italian crane.

Some time before, Reiver had been invited by the director to go with him to see how the repairs to the framework were going on, and that visit was a time when Reiver himself had found the present and the past intermingling in a disconcerting—or at least surprising—manner.

It had been during a mild spell in the middle of the previous December that, standing in a Berkshire field, he had looked down at the framework of wood laid out on the grass. Winter had not yet closed down on England. The sky was blue, the air gentle, the grass still green, the giant framework was all the blacks and browns and shining golds of English oak.

Some of it was oak cut down in the year 1360, and some was cut in the year 1991. For more than six hundred years the fourteenth-century framework had stood in the centre of the city for which it was made, the capital of the North Countrie, the ancient city of York, until, mismanaged by the years, cut where it was not meant to be cut and pierced where it was not meant to be pierced, it had tottered and bent and been condemned as a dangerous structure.

It might, all unheeding, have been swept away.

He had been greatly moved by the spectacle

of the giant framework, three storeys of medieval timber from the front of an old hall which no one had realized was there.

All over the framework men were working, expert carpenters. Pieces of oak destined to form arch braces lay over the upright and horizontal beams which they would join diagonally at the corners, while men marked them carefully in the places where a mortice and tenon joint must be cut, to the tiny tolerance of a few millimetres, not that they had millimetres in the fourteenth century.

'Parts have gone missing,' said the master carpenter standing next to Reiver on his right. 'Probably because doors had been driven through or new windows. Some of it had rotted because as the ground level gradually rose outside the building—to the height of a metre if you remember, Dr Reiver—damp earth came into contact with the walls. Some of it had other damage due to stresses and strains far more than it had been designed to bear, when the old stone wall used as foundation bowed and gave way under the weight of the structure.'

'You've replaced all that.'

'Yes, we've replaced it as they would have done, using oak we've selected.'

Reiver had heard about the search for the oak, the infinite care and patience taken in selecting the individual pieces as if a violin was being built. The massive structure before them had the same need for care as a musical instrument, for the attuning of one piece of wood to another, so that the building would form an organic whole as if it had grown that way with walls and floors and roof, the frame forming its skeleton which like a living creature could face the elements and learn to adjust its stresses if part of itself suffered change.

'How did you know what to put in the gaps where the structure had more or less vanished?' he asked.

'They told us.'

'Who told you?'

'The men who designed it in the first place.'

Reiver said nothing until he had thought about this.

'You mean the housewrights of 1360?' He knew that he sounded incredulous. What did the man mean? Was he going round the bend? He hoped no one was paying good money for some kind of occult intelligence obtained from psychic researchers.

'Housewrights,' said the director reflectively from where he stood on Reiver's left. 'I like that word. The parallel to cartwrights, makers of carts out of wood, and shipwrights, the makers of oaken ships. That's what this firm is. Perhaps they ought to use that on their letterheads. "Housewrights, medieval timber frames a speciality."'

'So how did the housewrights of 1360...'

'Come over here,' the master carpenter said.

As the three men bent over a blackened beam the carpenter pointed to three lines cut in the timber, a small diagonal line joining one of them, and certain other fine surface cuts which Ralph Reiver would hardly have noticed unless his attention had been drawn to them.

'You see those?'

'Yes.'

'They are instructions from the man who designed this building and in whose yard this frame was first assembled. Such buildings were prefabricated, did you know that? Then taken to pieces again and reassembled on site. Each timber of the hundreds was marked. This one says, "This is the third bay at the front, put a brace here." As it happens we know what the braces were like, partly because some survive and partly because they were pretty standard. So what I told you is true; the master carpenter of 1360 tells us what to do, we carry out his instructions.'

Ralph stood upright and drew back from the frame. He half closed his eyes and looked at the scene through blurred vision. The men in jeans and shirts moved as their kind have moved for ever. They carried out at the end of the twentieth century the instructions left by a boss who had died, no doubt, before the year 1400 came to England. They patiently replaced timber which was lost or irretrievably damaged from that maker's design and the whole thing made Ralph's toes tingle somehow with the feeling that time itself was only the flick of an eyelid.

'It's creepy,' he said to the director. 'It makes me feel quite peculiar. I anticipate that, after this, anything might happen, and probably will.'

The other man laughed. 'It is only common sense,' he said.

'Prefabricated,' Ralph Reiver said again. 'You mean that all over England were places where they took the trees after felling them in the forests, then they cut them up as required by the building which they were making, then marked them before taking them to pieces again and sending them off to be assembled on site by another firm, according to instructions ... Like painting by numbers or making Meccano.'

'A bit more skilled than that.'

'Standardized, he said about the braces.'

'That's right. I expect they were making one building after another. When you are doing that components tend to become standardized. You can imagine him, can't you, taking the order from his client—probably the building firm on the spot. "Four bays, sir? Right. The site is thirty feet wide ... Right ... Three storeys? Certainly, sir. What about decoration? A tasteful bit of carving, now ... Chamfered. Yes, no problem. Chamfering on the main ceiling beams, certainly, sir. We'll have it with you by next spring. Might even do

98

it for Martinmas if we are lucky with the timber and the weather." Probably it went like that,' said Ralph's companion, dropping back into his normal voice. 'But don't forget that although the principle is, as you said, as straightforward as painting by numbers these are highly sophisticated buildings, and if their inhabitants hadn't messed them about over the years they would have stood for ever.'

'They must be pretty heavy.'

The master carpenter passed him a piece of sawn timber about a foot square and some two inches thick. Ralph Reiver's hands did not expect it to be quite as heavy—they dropped a few inches in surprise.

'Now think how heavy those beams are,' the director said. 'A foot thick and some of them thirty feet long.'

* * *

Ralph Reiver, walking along Bootham and busy remembering that day in the previous December, bumped straight into a woman with a baby in a buggy. The buggy caught him a glancing blow on the ankle which almost made him cry out and the woman's several plastic bags full of shopping collided more centrally with his body.

'Why don't you look where you're going?' cried the woman angrily.

'So sorry, madam ... Is the baby all right?'

'No thanks to you.'

'No, of course—I really am so sorry.'

'Silly bastard,' the woman muttered to her companion as they walked on. 'Wasn't looking where he was going at all. I wouldn't like to be in a car he was driving.'

'No, well, I was telling you, Sally, about this top I saw in Fenwick's...'

*   *   *

The scene of crime officers had covered in the place where the scuffle—or fight—had taken place two nights previously on the top storey of the three-storey scaffolding. The timber frame was to be assembled when the crane had been set up and could bring in the timbers over the rooftops. The scaffolding was open to the elements except where the team had draped polythene. As the snowflakes fell on the Thursday they had hurried with the sheets of plastic to protect the area. Now they and Acting DS Bob Southwell stood round looking at it, uncovered once more.

'It's been photographed of course,' one officer said.

'This is the key area, then. The yard hadn't much to tell you.'

'There was so much dust,' replied another officer. 'Masses of footprints making just a dusty blur in most places. We photographed for the record. Up the stairs to this level, again

100

plenty of dust on the treads, but not nearly as much as in the yard. It was possible in places to separate some footmarks. Out here on these scaffold boards, relatively few distinct footmarks. Altogether there's so much dust on the site it's pretty hopeless. This morning when the building workers are interviewed the PCs are explaining that it's essential to eliminate them from involvement—I think they will appreciate that. We've asked that their footwear be checked, but it is a wild-goose chase actually.'

'If they were wearing the same shoes on Wednesday?'

'Exactly, sir. Most likely they will be—people usually only have one pair of work shoes at a time.'

'I'm sure they do. But during the evening they would be wearing something different, and in view of the dust is it worth spending time on footwear?'

'It might be useful. The questionnaires are a continuing process of course. It will be two weeks at least before that part of the enquiry is completed.'

'I think you're in two minds, officer. There are so few visible footmarks, which might not be relevant anyway, that you appear to be wasting time, but on the other hand, having found enough to identify some slight traces of the victim, you are hanging on like a bulldog and collecting evidence.'

The man smiled and said nothing.

'So what do you still have to do here?'

'We need to examine every surface for fibres. The samples we take on tape then go for forensic examination as you know, sir. We've defined the area under search and added a margin. A second pair of shoes has been identified in the area. The edges of the treads of the stairs, and one or two traces out here.'

'So it might be worth the time after all. You found traces in the area where he walked straight forward from the stair head and then began to stand, shuffle, ultimately fight?'

'Sir.'

'As you began with the yard outside and the passageways, we agreed yesterday that you'd finished there?'

'Yes, sir. The builders are using all that area now, but we've kept them out of this range so far.'

'Was there blood up here? I can't see any.'

'There is a splash, sir, on this upright scaffolding pole, look . . .' Carefully the officer moved over to one of the poles where the outer wall would be and indicated the splash.

'And that part next to where you're standing is where he fell over, right?'

'We think so, sir. If he'd been a short man the safety bar would have stopped him falling, but being tall, his hips probably sort of swivelled over it. Normally of course this area is perfectly safe.'

102

'Wouldn't the blood have positively sprayed out after the blow, marking everything up here within yards?'

'We think his clothing checked the outward rush of blood. Different from an exposed part of the body.'

'What about the assailant's clothes? Stained?'

'Could have been, if he was close. He must have been within arm's length anyway. We think probably some staining. We understand from the forensic reports that most slashes with the knife didn't draw blood, it was only one which did the damage. It seems fair to postulate that that was the last blow.'

'Then in a matter of seconds, probably, Followes was going over the edge?'

'We think so, otherwise there should have been blood on the boards up here.'

'Mmmm.' Bob looked thoughtfully round. 'If you haven't checked the whole area for footprints and fibres and anything else, you must check it all before handing it over. The thing to do—before the crane arrives—is to ask the builders exactly where they will need to be and go over that part first, then tape it off and proceed with the rest relatively at leisure. The other range ought to be covered thoroughly, too, although people are now working in it. When do you think you'll be finished?'

The first officer spoke again. 'There aren't as many complications, sir, as in a house. It

103

shouldn't take as long.'

'Dare I say two o'clock today? Only for the part you will be releasing for their use?'

The scene of crime officers looked at one another and at their watches.

'We can try.'

'Good lads. I'll see about getting impressions of the shoes of the others, too—the other duty archivist and his pal, then Followes' house-mate and girlfriend. May as well.'

CHAPTER SIX

Mr and Mrs Followes would think, years afterwards, that going to see their murdered son was the worst experience they had ever had to undergo. It was one of those events which are so much beyond normal life, which strike so deep into innermost feelings and fundamental emotions, that the minutes involved seem to be on another plane outside time. They hardly knew how they managed to exist through it. George's face was peaceful, his left hand no longer outflung, his body lay straight beneath its white covering, no wound was visible, the right hand was tucked under the cover. The chill of the mortuary struck into their hearts, and the sensations of being there were to haunt their dreams.

When they returned to their guest house the policewoman who had gone with them persuaded them both to take a little soup for their lunch, and drink a cup of tea with something comforting in it. It was as well she had done so, for they had still to face their questioning by Bob Southwell.

Bob arrived to join the policewoman at about two o'clock. He was gentle and sensitive in his approach to them, but it would hardly have mattered if he had been curt and abrupt, they barely felt his manner.

'The main thing is to give me a picture of your son,' he said. 'Tell me about his life, how his interests and career developed, what friends he had, how often you saw him of late, anything that comes into your heads.'

Once they started talking, they were able to carry on; the policewoman, who was Sarah Doughty, a friend of Jenny Wren's, sat in the background taking notes as fast as she could, and Bob dotted down an occasional note himself.

It was a familiar tale. Mr and Mrs Followes had had two children, a boy and a girl; the girl had married young, a nice man; the couple lived near them, and their daughter had two children herself. She was keeping an eye on the house while they were away, looking after the dog and putting food down for the cat.

Bob, and Sarah also, felt glad that the older couple would have support when they went home.

Their son, though, had been the pride of their hearts, with his progress through school to university. They might have preferred him to become an accountant or a teacher, but he had interested them in archaeology and they had given him every encouragement in his choice of a career.

'He seemed to be settled and happy here in York working for the Trust,' his father said.

'With Sophie, too,' his mother put in. 'She's coming to see us this afternoon.'

'I'm pleased about that,' murmured Bob. 'She's terribly upset, of course. It will help her to see you.'

'We thought, you know … he might write books about the digs … his essays were always so good. He might have been offered a lecturing post at a university or a teaching post at a college.'

'His life was in front of him,' said Mrs Followes.

At Bob's prompting, they went on to talk about George's friends, those from school he was still in touch with, the new ones he had made at various points in his life. Sarah Doughty in the corner scribbled industriously at her notes.

'Now, about his beliefs,' Bob urged gently. 'Was he religious? What were his politics? I'm trying to get at the things he felt deeply about.'

It appeared that George had not been a

regular attender at any kind of worship.

'We go to the local church occasionally,' Mr Followes said. 'Easter and Christmas, and if there's anything special on, like Harvest Supper.'

They didn't think he was active politically; they certainly weren't themselves, taking the most middle-of-the-road newspaper and deciding how to vote each time on the basis of the manifestos of the parties.

'Not political,' wrote Sarah Doughty.

It was archaeology he cared about, both George's parents said. One thing that made him really hot under the collar was those people with those metal detector things. He said there was a place for their use in proper digs at times but people were vandals when they went round the country any old where, not keeping proper records, probably not always declaring their finds, destroying the sites and the evidence as often as not.

'I had the impression things were much better regulated now,' Bob remarked. 'Aren't they much more responsible than some of them were at first? I thought those particular problems were sorted out, about over really.'

Apparently George was still not happy about the situation. But it was wider than that, Bob found. Lately, this worry and disturbance of his—although he hadn't said anything, they had the feeling that whatever was troubling him was in the same area.

It was the tone of his voice, according to Mrs Followes. She could tell that it was something of the same kind because there was only one thing that had ever brought that inflection into his voice. So although he'd denied there was anything wrong, she'd remembered overnight that it was the inflection which kept coming and going in his voice, when he thought of whatever it was that was troubling him, that was the same as when he talked about metal detectors.

Bob left them with more expressions of sympathy and long handshakes. He thought of his own son and daughter and how he would feel if . . . and within a few seconds had to stop that train of thought, it was too painful even to contemplate.

'You'll stay, Sarah?' he asked as the policewoman accompanied him to the door. 'I'll square it with your super. The girlfriend is coming along this afternoon; you might stay with them if you can, in a friendly way, but don't push it if you're not welcome. If you can stay with them, keep your ears open for anything useful that surfaces in conversation. Later, you could give them a hand organizing a taxi to the station—in fact why not go as far as seeing them on the train? It won't take too long.'

He was glad that Mr and Mrs Followes were going home to Cumbria. It was the best place for them, with their dog and cat and daughter,

108

son-in-law and grandchildren, until the time at last came for the release of their son's body. The waiting was the worst. Strange how important it was, the possession of the beloved body, the interment or cremation, the gravestone or other memorial put up in a suitable spot. Then at last the real grieving process could begin.

*   *   *

Once more it was latish when Bob set out for home, leaving a team working in the incident room. Work would be going on round the clock, writing up the results of interviews, entering them on the computer.

The children were still up when he reached Ouse Avenue and went in at his own front door. Fleetingly Bob thought of his friend and neighbour, Tom Churchyard, who lived in the attached house. They were all semi-detached along Ouse Avenue. Bob and Tom hadn't had their usual Thursday evening out at the local pub. Linda had cancelled it on behalf of Bob; Tom was very good about it, such cancellations had happened before. They'd make up for it when the case was over, thought Bob wearily as he stepped over his threshold into his small daughter's bunny hug.

'Still up, honey chile?' asked Bob as he swung Susan into his arms. She was in nightie and dressing-gown and smelt deliciously of

109

soap and talcum powder. Paul, his son, appeared in the sitting-room doorway, wearing his pyjamas.

'We've been watching telly, Dad,' he explained.

'At this time of night? What about school tomorrow morning?'

'We don't go to school on Saturdays, silly,' Susan said into his ear. Bob shook his head to free his ear from the tickle and blew into one of her ears in retaliation. Her long silky hair flew up in front of his breath.

'Take them up to bed, Bob, would you, dear?' asked Linda from the kitchen. 'I'm serving your meal. There's a letter.'

'Come on, you two villains.' Bob put Susan down and grasped a hand of each child. 'Let's see if we can go upstairs in giant steps. Who can do it in the least number?'

'It's not fair, your legs are longer, Daddy,' said Susan.

'I won't compete, I'll stop you two from falling.'

So with giant strides up the hill to Bedfordshire the children went, laughing and squealing. They were really too old for such nonsense but still loved it at times.

The children settled down quickly. Bob resisted their demand for stories, on the grounds that they'd been up for ages watching telly. He was on fire to go downstairs again; Linda had said there was a letter, and from the sound of her voice he knew what sort of letter she meant.

His throat constricted at the sight of the brown envelope.

'I didn't want to break your concentration by ringing to tell you about it,' Linda said. 'You had the media interview this morning and all the rest of the enquiry. I knew you'd rather wait until you reached home.'

He picked the letter up, then the knife she had laid for him, and slit the top open. Linda paused in her serving and watched him.

'I'm on the short list,' he said at last, hoarsely. 'I'm in with a chance, Lindylou.'

They gazed at one another across the gleaming white formica kitchen table. Another step in the process towards possible promotion safely negotiated.

'Of course I knew you would be,' she said confidently. 'Shall we have a bottle of wine?'

'Yes.'

He sat down, heavily. She had obviously eaten with the children, there was only one place set. He rested his head on his clasped hands. Linda reappeared carrying a bottle, then passed it to him, with a corkscrew. She took two tall-stemmed glasses from the cupboard, stood them on the table and seated herself opposite Bob.

'I'll toast your future,' she said, 'my superintendent.'

'Not that, Lin. Don't you do anything of the

kind. We'll toast my good luck in reaching the short list.'

'We always knew you would,' she said as they clinked glasses.

* * *

Friday night, which George and Sophie had always spent together. Sophie had seen Mr and Mrs Followes off on the train earlier; they would be nearing home by now. She looked round her flatlet and hated it. Everything in it reminded her of evenings spent with George. There was nobody she wanted to see and nothing she wanted to do. As soon as she decently could she had a hot bath and went to bed, lying there sipping a warm drink well laced with whisky, and reading the lightest novel she could find. Somehow it was midnight before she turned off the bedside lamp.

She woke abruptly and lay gazing into the darkness. The block of accommodation owned by the university was quiet; no gurgling water pipe broke the stillness, no gust of wind rattled the window pane, no drops of rain beat against the glass, nor did any snowflake softly swish across it.

Sophie switched on the light, brought her notebook closer on her night table, and began to write.

'We arrived back in England secretly from our exile, at Ravenspur, to find a country hostile and ruled once more by Henry VI and supporters of the Lancaster party. It was late at night, and where Richard Duke of Gloucester and his men were, none knew. Our hearts nearly failed us, but King Edward, bright and cheerful as ever, showed no sign of fear. Things looked better in the morning; before dawn the Duke arrived with his men—they had landed more to the north. Then we set out inland, on a course nor'-nor'-west, hoping to rest a day in the town of Kingston-upon-Hull, but they shut the gates and would not admit us. So there was nothing for it but to go on marching, resting when and where we could, wishing for the shipload of horses we'd lost on the voyage, and when we reached Beverley they let us in, and good refreshment we had there. Our speed was as fair as we could expect, with only one load of horses left for our small army; some days we made fifteen miles, some we didn't, sometimes we managed a little more. It was very late on the day we reached York, longing to enter the city for a good night's sleep, that was when we had the worst shock. We have been in the city of York often enough since Towton, and the people have seemed complacent to us, but now when we stand outside the gates cold and hungry and longing for a decent bed, they will not let us in. Edward, his head thrown back to look up at the mayor as he stands high in a window of the Walmgate Bar, has to plead for admittance. They know they have the upper

113

hand. They are still in favour of King Henry, with the old reverence for his anointing, in spite of Edward's crowning and nigh ten years of his good government. His treatment of the city after Towton still rankles. I could put an arrow through the mayor and that would stop his nonsense but no, we are to win them round through Edward's schemes and his golden tongue.

Richard, the young Duke of Gloucester, has been saying, "Let us go on, leave it, brother, we should not dissemble, I will not be party to a pretence," but Edward answered him roughly at first, saying, "Is not your first care to your men? Have you led them over the peril of the sea only to have them sleep in ditches and under hedges when within York is accommodation for all of us?" Then, putting his arm affectionately round the lad's shoulders, he cozened him, speaking softly so that we who stood by could hardly hear, "Come, brother, this is statecraft, sometimes it is necessary to deceive, come, stand by me in this."

Now Richard is at his side as Edward shouts up to the mayor, "I intend only to retrieve my own Duchy, good sir, we mean no harm to Henry. He has never been hurt by Yorkist hands. Come, do you not see we wear the ostrich plumes of Lancaster?" and where he found those feathers blest if I know, but, by Our Lady, there he has them on his helm.

114

Now they believe us—or say they do. Look, they are unbarring the gate. No, the army is not to be admitted; the king and duke and a handful of men, we of the bodyguard, may pass in, the rest are to remain outside.

King Edward strides forward with his long free pace, few of us are as tall as he, he sets a sharp speed on a march. Richard, so much shorter and slighter, has all on to keep up. Edward, as he goes, is shouting that all York may hear (and they say there are twelve thousand people living in the city), "Henry! Henry!" His shouts ring through the silent streets. I notice Richard Duke of Gloucester shouts not, yet gazes from side to side as if he was glad, right glad, to see York again. The people stand mute to see our little band pass by. We few men, who went in boldly, bear ourselves proud as popes, and the mayor and the aldermen are so impressed with the king and duke's friendliness and presence that they relent and open the gates wide and invite in all the rest of our army, for which they are thankful and praise God and keep on shouting out, "Henry! Henry!" now and again, so as to remind them that we are no rebels against the good man Henry. There is more arguing to do yet, but Edward will win, as he always does, and before long we will have warm beds tonight and good bread and meat and good ale.

If when this campaign is done, we are still alive, which God grant, and if Edward has the mastery, as he will I doubt not, he is born to twist people to his way, the service of Richard the Duke is for me if I can get it, for I love the stance he took for true-seeming and against this mummery.'

Sophie shivered. The March night was as drear and cold as any night had been in the fifteenth century. She put down her ball-point and climbed out of bed, switching on the electric wall heater and fetching her dressing-gown to wrap around her. She peeped through the curtains but saw no reason to keep them open and closed them again firmly against the darkness.

It was caused by Dr Reiver, she thought, with his talk of Edward and Richard, and how Edward had been like Mark Antony in reverse—or had that been her own suggestion? —for it was not long afterwards that Edward had poor Henry VI put to death in the Tower of London when his usefulness was over. When Edward entered London on 21st May 1471 he had Queen Margaret as part of his triumphal procession, dragged in a chariot to taste the full humiliation of defeat, her only son dead, and a couple of days later another procession came from the Tower of London with her husband's body, bearing it to St Paul's. The report was that the corpse bled on the pavement in St Paul's and again at the church of Black Friars on its way to burial. Miraculous, it was said at the time, for dead men do not bleed. Perhaps

116

the murdered king, only his face uncovered, was not quite dead...

What a politician that man Edward was. If he had lived there was no way Henry Tudor could have come to the throne. Perhaps Edward won in the end, after all. Dog breeders say if you want to know how a pup will turn out, look at the maternal grandsire; and Henry VIII was the image of his grandfather Edward IV, in character too. Sophie sat by the heater, and the thoughts that rang through her brain were of manipulation, and treachery, and double-dealing, and betrayal.

*   *   *

On the Saturday morning all the police staff working on the murder at Barley Hall were in at work as if it were a weekday. So were the workmen, preparing for the coming of the special crane. As he made his way up the stairs to the incident room, Bob Southwell was behind two of the girls who worked higher up.

'Has anyone interviewed the girls who work in the Trust's office?' he asked the woman sergeant who was in charge of the computer work.

'I'm sure they have. Let's check ... Yes. Shall we run you off a copy of the interviews?'

'It's all right—who did them? I'd rather have a quick word.'

The sergeant bent over the computer screen.

'Mr Smart,' she said after a moment.

'Thanks. I expect he's around somewhere.'

Bob ran Dave Smart to earth outside, chatting to DI Rollo about the scene of crime team's progress.

'Don't let me interrupt,' he said, but the other two stopped talking at once.

'We've finished—all right, John?' said Dave.

'Fine. Morning, sir,' and John Rollo went inside the scaffolding and up the old flight of stairs to where the scene of crime team was working.

'You needn't have broken it up,' reproached Bob.

'We'd finished anyway. I was about to come back inside the office.'

'You interviewed the Trust's office staff, I take it?'

'Yesterday, boss. They weren't in on Thursday—the director contacted them and gave them the day off. They're in today to make up for it. Was there a query?'

'I wondered whether anyone had remembered to speak to them. I certainly hadn't thought of it, until just now when I saw two of them as I went upstairs. Tell me about the interviews. Save me reading the report and I'd rather have it from the horse's mouth anyway.'

'There are three girls working there. They are raising funds for the Barley Hall project, and doing the publicity, telling everyone who is taking an interest what is happening, what's planned, and so on.'

'Did they know the victim?'

'Yes, but they don't seem to have been close. They saw both Followes and Lleyn whenever they were on duty, at coffee time, lunchtime, that kind of thing.'

'Work colleagues, then.'

'Yes.' Dave went on telling Bob about the three interviews, giving him all kinds of insights which he might not have found in the report. After a while they both went on their different ways, but Bob had decided he would like to talk to the girls in the office himself. The next time he was climbing the stairs he went up the extra flight, knocked on their door and went in, introduced himself, and in general caused disruption.

'I'd be grateful if you would explain to me what the object of the project is,' he said at last. 'The outlines I know of course, but...'

The tallest and slimmest of the girls offered to talk to him about it, and they went downstairs and out into the crowded courtyard.

'Explain it to me,' asked Bob. 'What are you going to do with it when it's been reconstructed?'

'We're going to make it a living medieval household,' the girl explained, with excitement in her voice. 'You might call it a living history museum, but museum is a stuffy word. The

119

rooms are going to be reconstructed the way they were then. Our historical adviser has been researching the period and he's been discovering what people had in their houses and everything. We aren't going to put in old things, medieval things, but modern replicas made in the same way they were then, to the same patterns. We don't want it to be a static museum but like a living household of the time. It's thrilling, really. There's talk of having people in the roles of members of the household, recreating the life. We're choosing, not the time when it was first built, but slightly later when it was leased to a goldsmith who was a Lord Mayor of York. The mayor and aldermen were very important in those days, they ran the city. At this end of Stonegate the goldsmiths congregated. They worked in silver too, mainly in silver we think, although they called themselves goldsmiths. The man who leased what is now Barley Hall was William Snowshill, or Snawsell. As you know, spelling wasn't standard then. His next-door neighbour was another goldsmith, from Germany, called John of Cologne. There are amazing wills from that period with inventories which go through every room in the house telling you exactly what's in it. They even included things like broken birdcages and bundles of rags.'

'Really?' Bob reflected that people didn't make wills and inventories like that nowadays. 'You mean going in the door of Barley Hall is going to be like stepping back into the fifteenth century, as if the building had been miraculously transported to today?'

'That's it. As far as we can make it, it really will be time travel. Only they're having modern loos for the visitors.'

'And for the re-enactors playing the family too, I hope,' joked Bob.

'Well, yes. And the water will be from York Water Company, not straight from the river.'

'Very sensible. But the water in our taps does come from the Ouse, doesn't it?'

'Not direct, it's purified first. The two-storey range will be the Great Hall which was the general living and eating place, and the kitchens, pantry and buttery. The hall will go right up to the roof, the other rooms will have chambers over. The fire for living round will be on a central hearth in the middle of the floor of the Great Hall. They'll have another fire in the kitchen for cooking, I think.'

'That's what the little turret on the roof is for, to let out the smoke?'

'Yes.'

'My wife was thrilled by the roof.'

'It is lovely, isn't it?'

As he stood by the side of this graceful, elegant girl, Bob suddenly felt he could see through her eyes how it was all going to be.

Instead of the clutter of a building site he saw a comely cobbled yard with pleasant buildings on two sides. He saw people in sweeping cloaks

121

and spreading gowns walking to and fro, the servants of the household busy with besoms and wooden buckets, the apprentices and journeymen inside bending over their jewellers' pegs with their work, leather aprons under the pegs catching the tiniest fragment or filing of precious metal as it fell during the process of making. He saw others with their hammers raising silver from sheet form to create nobly shaped tankards and vessels for use in the service of God, for the forty churches of the crowded surrounding city.

'I think you're planning something really rather wonderful,' he said.

The rest of the day passed quickly for the police involved and for the building workers. Outside their secluded area, the city seethed with Saturday shoppers. Normally this would have been reflected in Coffee Yard by a stream of people passing along the alleyway and pausing to peep at the work going on, but the police were still strictly controlling access. It looked as though the work of the famous crane would be able to start on time, after all. Then, for the scheduled three-week period, the public would still be strictly excluded for their own safety.

Progress was being made with the enquiries; slow but satisfying progress.

CHAPTER SEVEN

Saturday was more eventful for others equally involved in the case.

Sophie took a telephone call in the morning which surprised and disturbed her.

'Marius here,' said George Followes' house-mate. 'Will you do something for me, Sophie?'

'If I can,' she answered, wondering what it could be.

'Can you come and sort out and pack George's stuff?'

'What do you mean?'

'I don't see why I should have to do it. There will be things of yours, probably, or things he would have wanted you to have that his parents won't want. The rest are going to be sent back to them.'

'But Marius, what's the hurry? Goodness, he only died on Thursday.'

'Late Wednesday night, they think,' said the precise Marius.

'Whenever. What's the hurry, I asked you?'

'I need to replace him. I must have the income from that room, and it'll need redecorating I expect. Luckily he didn't die there, or no one would have wanted to rent the place at all.'

Sophie stood staring at the telephone.

'Are you still there, Sophie?'

'Yes.'

'Can you come over, or can't you?'

'I'll come.' She looked at her watch. 'Will ten o'clock suit you?'

'If you can't make it earlier.'

Sophie had thought nothing Marius did could surprise her. Now she burned with indignation. Callous beast. How could he ask her to do any such thing? But at last, having drunk a mug of fresh strong coffee laced with brandy to strengthen her nerves, she began to think that she'd rather carry out the task than have Marius's ugly mitts on anything which had belonged to George. Then she thought she'd better put George's parents in the picture.

Her voice was wavering and apologetic on the phone to Cumbria. She wanted to consult them. This was what had happened, and she felt she had to comply, but what did they want her to do? What did they want to happen to George's clothes, for instance?

'Do you want us to come down and help?' asked Mr Followes.

'No, no, you've only just got back home.'

'It's good of you, Sophie. We can't think what the fellow is playing at. My wife's in tears here.'

Sophie was nearly in tears herself.

Mrs Followes came on the phone. 'As far as the clothes go, dear, a charity, don't you think so? I couldn't bear to have them sent here and at least they'll do someone some good.' Then she began to cry again, and Mr Followes came back on.

'Sophie, anything of George's which you can use in your work we'd like you to have. Books, for instance. As for his notebooks, can you look through them and give us your opinion as to whether anything ought to be published? You'll know far better than we will.'

'It would be good to publish something if we could.'

'As a memorial,' said George's father.

'Yes indeed,' and if anyone's going to prepare and organize that, I want it to be me, thought Sophie.

By ten o'clock she was knocking on the door of the street house in the Groves.

'Have the police had a look round?' she asked when Marius unlocked the door of George's bed-sit and showed her in. It didn't look as it used to do. Not all upside-down exactly, but there was a mist of powder here and there which made her think of fingerprinting, and nothing seemed quite the way she remembered.

Marius drew the curtains further back from the windows to let in more of the March light.

'They came Thursday, and again yesterday,' he said. 'I was at work yesterday so I don't know how long they stayed then. They went right through the house. I had said they could. Now I want George's things cleared out of

125

this room.'

Sophie stiffened. 'Some of his things will be in the rest of the house,' was all she said.

'Right. I'll go through and check and bring everything to you in here. The locks will have to be changed. *Anyone* might have a key.'

He closed the door quickly behind him or Sophie would have lashed out at this. How dare he suggest she would use her key to enter the house as and when she liked, for that was what he had been implying. Did he expect her to come stealing? For that was what he had been implying also. She hated him for all the possible meanings of his remark, but decided it would be beneath her dignity to answer it, or pick a quarrel. Then it seemed good to her that everything belonging to George should be out of this place as soon as she could manage it.

She had come prepared with knapsack and plastic carrier bags as well as her usual soft round basket, to take away as much as she could. Swiftly she packed George's everyday clothes and then his few good ones separately, checking in case he'd left anything in the pockets.

Marius opened the door and dumped George's dirty clothing in a pile on the floor then shut the door again. Really, he was making the whole thing impossibly sordid. He must have found these things in the linen basket or the washing machine. She'd wash them at home before giving them away. Tears

126

had been flowing for some time and when she picked up the jersey George had been wearing the previous week and caught the scent of him, her hanky and the jersey became soaked together. She pulled the woolly over her head and pushed her arms into it, feeling for one last time as if she was in his embrace.

This won't do, she thought to herself. Nor can I carry everything, and there's his desk and computer. I need a small removal van.

'Don't forget to leave the money for the call,' Marius said as he saw her using the Yellow Pages directory to find someone to help with a small removal on a Saturday morning without notice.

Even nowadays miracles sometimes happen. She found a firm willing to help. They also sent some cardboard boxes, and a tea-chest or two.

After about an hour's hard work for Sophie and the young man who came with the van, the room was empty of everything except the bed and other fittings which had been there when George took possession. After stowing the last items in the overflowing van, Sophie went back into the house, back into the room, and stood silently looking around at the bare bones of the place where she had often been happy, sitting talking, drinking coffee, dreaming or reading while George typed notes into the computer, making love. She lost count of time.

Marius came in at the door, roughly disturbing her silent farewell.

'Good,' he said as he looked around. 'The van driver's getting impatient out there and I haven't all day, either. You'd better give me your key and go, Sophie.'

Her face was as white and hard as stone as she fished in her bag for the key and for some change for the phone calls she had made to removal companies.

'Goodbye,' he said as she went out of the front door, but she did not even move her head to look at him, until suddenly she turned and threw the key and the money for the phone in his face.

Sophie was so short that even climbing into the cab of the small van presented her with a difficulty, but the driver leaned over and held out a hand, hoisting her in beside him. After faltering out directions to her flat, she dissolved into tears, and wept all the way. She was glad that the driver appeared to take no notice.

Behind, Marius stood in the empty room and told himself how pleased he was. He examined the carpet, which showed quite clearly where desk, chair, piles of books, and other possessions of George's had stood upon it. He went round the walls inspecting the marks where pictures had hung, where books had allowed dust to accumulate behind them. He took down the curtains and shoved them in the washer. He fingered Sophie's key where it lay in his pocket and felt brutally pleased with himself, angry, glad to be rid.

* * *

Next door, a police constable taking part in the enquiry was filling in a form with answers to questions.

'You did know Mr Followes, then, madam?'

'Oh, yes, him and his girlfriend, that Sophie. Nice girl.'

'Can you tell me if you noticed anything unusual on Wednesday?'

'They had a row, Mr Followes and Mr Caile. They often had a row. I could hear them through the wall.'

The constable wrote that down, carefully. 'What time was that?'

'About half-past six.' The neighbour nodded self-righteously. She was careful never to have rows with anyone. This questioning filled her with self-importance. These young people needed showing up. Look what it came to. One young chap dead and his girl taking his stuff away with tears running down her face. She'd tell them what was what.

* * *

Other constables were checking on the workforce of the building project, either wandering round the busy men on site getting in their way, or else knocking at the doors of their homes. The task was still to enquire where they had been late on Wednesday night; how well had they known the dead man, what sort of person was he, did they know of anyone he was on bad terms with, could they see work shoes?

At Heslington others were checking with the university students, particularly the graduate students, some of whom had studied with George or Sophie. What was George's circle of friends, did they know him personally, did they know anyone who had cause to dislike him, did they know what it was that had been disturbing his peace of mind during the last weeks of his life?

*   *   *

The constable who had been sent to check on the alibis of Eliot Lleyn and his house-mate was out of luck. As he was entering the narrow residential road, a large camper-van was coming out of it, loaded with children and the impedimenta for holiday. The PC had to stop and wait until the camper had safely manoeuvred itself out through the two streams of traffic on the main road. Then when he reached the nearest neighbour, opposite Lleyn's house, there was no answer to his knock. The house looked thoroughly shut up. The neighbour across the narrow road answered her door.

'I don't see much of Eliot and his pal,' she explained. 'I work. Out at seven of a morning and not back until seven at night. Then I have a social life, you know? I don't hear them, not ever as far as I remember, unless they're having a party in the garden and that doesn't worry me. To be honest, you're lucky to have caught me. I'm never in!' She smiled roguishly. 'You want to ask the people the other side. They're matey with Eliot, but you won't get them now.'

'The house looks shut up,' said the constable.

'Well, they're only away for the weekend. They've gone to the coast. It's amazing you've missed them. They've only just gone. Did you see a big camper-van?'

The constable said he had.

'That was them. They'll be back late Sunday night, ready for Monday. You can ask them then.'

She nodded and shut the door in the constable's face. He reflected that for someone who was never in and knew nothing whatever about her next-door neighbours, she knew a lot about the family even farther away, the ones with the camper-van.

*   *   *

Sophie was back at her own flatlet, moving furniture so that the desk could be squeezed in and the computer put on it. The desk had been the first thing into the removal van, and so was the last thing out. Everything else was piled around on the floor, but she'd have plenty of time later to sort things out.

'Will you have a drink of tea before you go?' she asked the driver.

'Thanks.'

Standing with the mug of tea, he looked round the now crowded room. 'It's a lot of work for you, isn't it?' he said.

'I don't mind. Someone has to do it, his family are a long way off, and I'd rather it was me.'

'Funny beggar your boyfriend lived with, isn't he?'

'He is a bit,' said Sophie, who was too sore to want to talk about Marius. 'Can I pay you now or do I have to wait for a bill?'

'Our boss gave you a quote, didn't he?'

'He did,' said Sophie, naming the amount.

'Right. I can give you a receipt.'

She tipped him generously. He had been patient, thoughtful, kind, but impersonal. Sophie appreciated that, but she was glad when he had gone.

Then she looked round with something very like despair. Small walkways through the mounds of books and files were all the space she had to move in. She was still wearing George's woolly and decided to have a rest, lie down for an hour, just relax and try to forget it all. Pulling the duvet over her head, she tucked her nose down as near as it would go to her chest and deeply inhaled the scent of the woolly. Her eyelids shut. Without meaning to, she dozed.

* * *

In the Groves, the door was locked with a new lock, at the house which George and Marius had shared. There was no sound audible to the keen ears of the next-door neighbour who had been so helpful to the police. In the backyard scrap of garden, a cat who was chased out regularly now saw his chance and leapt down from the wall of the back lane. He had a most interesting time sniffing and scratching and digging holes and contributing to the organic nature of the garden's fertility. Long before the back door was opened again, he had become bored and jumped back on to the wall, answering the call of hunger pains and returning to his own home.

Inside the house it was fairly quiet, too. Marius was there, but he was lying on the stairs, as he had been for a couple of hours.

He was weeping silently into the stair carpet.

The carpet smelt dusty and when he opened his swollen eyelids for a few seconds he could see stains he had never noticed before, and hairs and fluffy bits which had escaped being vacuumed up for weeks. On the wall in one place was a faint veil of cobweb, and the tiny spider whose home it was.

CHAPTER EIGHT

It was the Sunday morning, and the Italian crane had arrived in the centre of York on the previous night. It was parked on the agreed spot in St Helen's Square. A private security firm kept an eye on it. Probably the Saturday night revellers wondered what on earth was happening.

On Sunday morning the cold spell of weather was still with them. No more snow, but there had been a keen frost. Bob's car windows were frozen up when he went out at eight o'clock. He and a select band of policemen were to be on duty at Barley Hall, in addition to the team still labouring away in the incident room above the shop in Stonegate.

After parking the car, Bob walked up Stonegate as he had walked on the previous Thursday morning. There was no rubbish skip now, but two of the builder's vans had to squeeze past several cars which were parked in the narrow street, near to Coffee Yard.

Building workers at the entrance to the alley stood in a group, drinking coffee. The lively woman photographer, who was recording progress for the architect, had arrived wearing a bright red jumper and black trousers. As Bob reached her she was obviously leaving.

'Coming back in ten minutes,' she smiled at him.

Inside the yard, half a dozen men in white hard hats were frantically busy. Bob presumed they were preparing for the arrival of the crane. They were sweeping with enormous brushes, picking up the least little thing which shouldn't be on the ground, such as odd nails, and removing clutter. They looked tired, and Bob knew that the builder had paid them to be on duty all night, catching up with the work lost through a day's complete idleness and half a day with only partial access.

A lot more scaffolding had gone up overnight. Joiners, bare-headed, were erecting a doorway to shut off Coffee Yard's entrance from Stonegate. The other entrance, the alley from Swinegate, had already been shut off. The band of uniformed policemen who would be on duty all day arrived.

Older men in hard hats and bright blue or orange overalls, new faces to Bob, arrived and helped with the clearing up. They were different types to the building workers and joiners he'd grown to recognize; bigger, burlier, rougher looking altogether. They had come with the crane.

An electric cart with a trolley was taken out of the yard—it made a sound like a cow in pain. One of the joiners told Bob that the cart was to bring the framework of the crane in pieces from St Helen's Square.

Looking round and trying to keep out of the way of the workmen, Bob thought what a lot of progress had been made since the day he and his family stood and watched. On the two-storey range, all the ground-floor spaces between the oak uprights were now filled in with building blocks. The architect had told him that the original filling was probably wattle and daub, later replaced by brick infill, but both would be too labour-intensive for the rebuild. Each era had filled the spaces with the material of its own day, and the blocks would be covered in the authentic way. The edges of the roof of the two-storey range were protected by sheeting of blue plastic.

The cart and trolley moaned their way back from St Helen's Square and brought into the yard pieces of wood and metal. The policemen and the photographer stood and watched the unloading. The photographer, Polly, had been back for some time and was taking shots of events. A drainage hole in the yard was now covered up, using some of the wood. Four of the new gang manhandled a large heavy metal cross from the trolley and placed it across the new cover of the drain.

Bob was rubbing his cold finger-ends. 'I'm going for a coffee,' he said to Polly. 'Would you like to come along?'

She said she thought it was a good idea. They walked off the site and down Stonegate until they reached St Helen's Square, where Betty's Café was already open, with only a handful of customers as yet. They took a table with a good view of what was going on outside. The hot fresh coffee was exactly what they needed after being in the open since early morning, and the moaning cart and trolley would not escape their notice when the next load was fetched from the artic parked in the square.

It was nearly ten o'clock before they returned to Barley Hall, and a church bell was ringing. Bob wondered why he had decided to come and spend his Sunday morning watching what was obviously going to be a very slow process. At least he was having an interesting talk to the photographer. She intended to take a lot of shots of the first range of building, for the open structure would soon be completely closed in. Spry and active, she almost ran up a slender shaking ladder to first-floor level, followed slowly by Bob. Through the oaken framework now enclosing them, they could look down at the men working in the yard.

Their own scene was more homely. Most of the first floor was bare and open, but a small area, a few feet across, next to the chimney stack, had been framed in and defended by sheets of polythene, and within was a cosy corner with chairs and general clutter strewn about, hammers, nails, bits of wood, a dustbin lid on one end of the table, wooden mouldings piled by the wall. The cosy corner had old

Marley tiles on the floor and there was an unlit paraffin heater. Architects' drawings lay on the table, and below it an old pair of boots had fallen over, abandoned.

Lengths of wood, heating panels, pieces of ply, lay around the open part of the floor, ready for the joiners on their next working day. A length of glass fibre insulation hung down from what would be the ceiling.

While the photographer roamed about taking shots, Bob stayed for a while in the sheltered corner, glad to be warmer than in the open. The brick fireplace arches attracted his attention. Both now empty of chimneypieces or grates, they backed on to opposite sides of the stalwart chimney breast made of early bricks—Bob might not be an architectural expert, but he knew these bricks were centuries old. He filled in his minutes tracing the lines of mortar idly with his finger, thinking about the history this thick mountain of bricks had seen.

It would have been hard to say when he noticed that one of the small half-bricks was loose in its mortar. He had been day-dreaming. Day-dreaming childishly, he scolded himself afterwards. Childishly enough to wriggle the loose brick as if it was a tooth, then finding his penknife and easing the blade in beside it, begin to move it outwards. The project became the most important thing in the world for his idle mind that Sunday morning. It took a while, but the brick was coaxed out eventually, and he felt a great surge of pleasure rush through him. He peered in as though the empty space was the mouth of a fairy cave.

There was nothing there. Bob couldn't help feeling disappointed, though nothing was exactly what he had been expecting. He felt in his pocket for the small pen-torch he sometimes carried since Christmas, when it had been a present from his son Paul. The slender beam of light moved round the squarish hole where the brick had been. Nothing, and again nothing. Except another hole. Also empty. A strangely shaped hole, and as his mature and adult mind woke from his idle childish day-dreaming, his eyes focused on that small strange depression in the back wall of the space where the brick had been.

'Polly!' he called to the photographer, keeping his voice flat and unexcited. He didn't want to give her a shock in case she was teetering on a swaying ladder to obtain a better viewpoint, or on the edge of one of those places where the floorboards weren't down yet.

Her voice came in reply from somewhere above and beyond the cosy corner he was standing in.

'Polly,' he shouted back in reply, 'can you take a photograph here for me?'

She announced that she wouldn't be a minute.

Breathless, she arrived back and grabbed her photographer's bag up from the floor.

'Have to change the film,' she said. 'Do you want colour or black and white, for a transparency or negative film? What is it you want taking?'

'Only this hole where this brick was. I want to put it back and you know what these archaeologists are. There's a little depression, a hollow, behind it—they're bound to want a record and soon this will all be rebuilt or plastered in, I expect. Anyway, I'd like them to tell me what made the funny little depression.'

She humoured him, taking out a flash bulb and going to as much trouble as if she was photographing the crown jewels, then taking a view of the whole chimney stack, showing the gap where the brick had been removed.

'Thanks,' he said. 'When can I have the prints?'

Flicking her dark hair back from her face, she looked at him in surprise. 'A couple of days. Is it important?'

Bob shrugged. 'I don't like unfinished things hanging about.'

'You can have the film if you like. I've taken just the two shots on it. The only point is, if it is used for publication, I would like the credit for my work.'

'It's unlikely to be for publication, though one never knows. Is that all right? Will you have plenty of film if I take this one?'

She was still looking at him as though he had changed into something else, something very surprising. Bob wondered what. A frog? He could of course have asked one of the police photographers to take the shots, but would have had to leave the brick out while he found them, or replace it and then take it out again. It was much more convenient asking Polly, while she was on the spot.

Now Bob found the small six-inch rule which was usually lurking in his inside pocket, and his notebook, and made a rough sketch of the hole and the depression, marking the measurements in millimetres as near as he could. Then he set about returning the brick to its space, carefully, as though doing it neatly and exactly would earn him the promotion he hoped for, even though at that moment promotion was the farthest thing from his thoughts. Soon the half-brick was back in place, among the mixture of brick which made up the chimney stack. He smoothed the surface fragments from the gritty surround with his penknife, trying to camouflage the traces of his activity. When Polly, still looking surprised, had gone back to her work, he scooped up dust from the floor and camouflaged some more.

When he was satisfied and went out of the corner into the open framework again, he looked down through a gap in the floor into the body of the medieval building. The cement mixer was down below, next to the large orange tool container. This usually stood with its lid up, but was now locked. The screens passage had been opened up and formed one enormous space with the original hall area. Walking about, Bob discovered that there was a triangular yard at the back of the range, due, he found later, to an octagonal Methodist chapel which once stood there.

By the time it was eleven Bob was fed up with idling about. The sun was now bright, even if not yet warm. Polly was taking photographs from the first-floor window of Thomas Gent's Coffee House, of the work taking place in the yard. Someone else was videoing from the top of the scaffolding, for the Trust. The foundation of the crane from Milan was now established: four square bases, one for each foot—legs extended from the original cross— fourteen baulks of concrete or stone on one side, twelve so far on the other, providing a weighty basis for the superstructure.

The yard was alive with workmen clearing up once more with brushes and shovels, putting the debris, loose dirt and scraps of wood into a barrow. They threw long pieces of wood and odd panels up to the first-floor level. Some were already knocking off for their lunch break, others were drinking coffee wherever they happened to be.

Bob went home.

First, though, he contacted his scene of crime officers, still busy in the three-storey range, and asked one of them to see that the roll of film was taken for developing. He checked in the incident room, too, and made sure that all was well and the work going smoothly. He remembered what Dave had said, that working a computer program was slower than manual work. That was how it seemed at times.

*   *   *

Sunday afternoon with no family within reach and the one you love dead and lying in a mortuary is not the jolliest time of the week. The city of York lay quietly in the cold sunshine of that spring, snowdrops still blooming in the gardens, daffodils pushing up their noses hesitantly into the light, forsythia not yet opening its buds.

Sophie, hardly able to move in her flatlet for the piles of George's belongings, knew that the other residents in the block would welcome her if she knocked on their doors, but she did not want their company. She sat by her table, gazing out at the garden of the old house which had been converted. Snuggling into the warmth of George's grubby old woolly, she drew her notebook towards her and opened its pages, then picked up her pen to continue the story which was haunting her. Dr Reiver thought it was a good idea. She would show it to him; he said he would come today.

The phone rang before she started, and when she answered it was the quiet, cultured voice of

Ralph Reiver.

'How are you, Sophie?'

'All right, I suppose. Were you coming round, Dr Reiver?'

'Sophie, it's sweet of you to be so formal, but perhaps you would call me Ralph. I can't come today, something has turned up—my daughter and her boyfriend have arrived unexpectedly. They're on their way north, touring by cycle, and will be going off first thing in the morning.'

'Something awful happened yesterday,' said Sophie.

'What?' Concern could be heard in his voice. She told him about Marius Caile's demand that George's things should be moved immediately, and how she had coped, and how she felt about it. She could almost see Ralph Reiver tighten his lips in anger, it was so clear in his suddenly constricted voice.

'Whatever was the man playing at?' he asked, and went on without waiting for an answer, 'I feel I must tell the police about this. Do you mind, Sophie?'

'I don't mind.'

'So what are you doing with the things?'

She explained.

'You should have contacted me, I could have helped.'

'That's all right.' How on earth could she have rung up a retired lecturer, she thought, and asked him to help with the removal? But it was nice of him to say that.

'I'm really sorry not to be able to see you today, Sophie, in these circumstances. Could you join me tomorrow for lunch in King's Manor? Would that suit you?'

Sophie said it would suit her very well, she was booked in to work at the City Archives in the morning. 'I've been carrying on with my writing,' she said a little hesitantly.

'That's splendid. Will you bring it with you? I'm looking forward to reading it, very much, and we'll talk over this peculiar business of Marius Caile.'

'I usually go to King's Manor about twelve o'clock,' said Sophie. 'Would that be all right for you?' She couldn't quite bring herself to call him Ralph.

'Exactly right. They have a good choice at that time. I'll see you there.'

Sophie put down the phone feeling happily reassured and pleased. It was almost better than having him come round. Having someone to share a meal with, someone who knew the trouble she was in and conveyed sympathy without being obtrusive, someone interested in this funny writing she was doing—that was what she needed at the moment.

She picked up her ball-point—Sophie's choice was always the wider ball, more free-flowing type—and began to write rapidly in her large round script, losing herself completely for the time being in something so long ago and yet to her so immediate.

145

On Monday morning Bob Southwell was called to see his chief.

'Congratulations on making the short list,' the chief said. 'We were sure you would, of course. Now, Bob, arrangements. As you know, the next stage is two days of interviews and assessments. The dates have come through. It's later this week.'

'That's short notice, sir!'

'There's nothing to wait for. All you short list candidates will be together, going over the same hurdles.'

Bob thought it sounded horrific, but his ambition was burning bright and he was willing to face anything.

'It isn't a very convenient time,' he reminded his chief. 'I'm in the middle of a murder enquiry. The one at Barley Hall.'

'No one could help knowing about that, Bob, it's hardly low profile. I'm sure, if you brief them properly, your team can carry on without you for two days.'

Bob didn't like this assumption at all, but it was a Catch 22 situation. If he said they couldn't manage, it was a reflection on his leadership and training. If he sounded too happy about them fending for themselves without him, it seemed as if he was dispensable.

His chief looked as though he was mind-reading. 'You can keep in touch by phone,' he

146

remarked. 'If they really need to ask you something, they can ring. It's only two days, after all. What would happen if you had flu or an accident? We haven't the budget to pay for cover, Bob, even for senior officers.'

'No, of course, sir. I suppose I'm rather wrapped up in the enquiry at the moment, that's all. Of course they'll manage perfectly well.'

'Good. That's settled, then. Here's the bumf they've sent through about the assessments.' He spread out a sheaf of papers on the desk top.

* * *

Twelve o'clock was striking in the Minster bell tower as Sophie Beans turned in from Exhibition Square to the grounds of King's Manor. The interesting buildings to her right, continuing the line of the Art Gallery in the square, and the older buildings at right angles to these and lying immediately in front of her, were a fantastic mixture of times and styles and even materials, but they blended harmoniously into a beautiful and tranquil scene. As she walked down the stone-flagged path towards the main entrance to this part of York University, she admired as she always did the tall hollies on the left of the path, their camellia-shaped leaves glittering in the cold air. The fringe of vegetation and the wall behind it effectively shut off the bustle of the street beyond.

Once the Minster chimes were over, telling the world that the hour was about to strike, Big Peter, the giant bell, took command. Sophie had heard that its clapper alone weighed three-quarters of a ton. Big Peter's voice could be heard over the nearby streets of the walled city; she listened now with joy and reassurance, even in the mist of her pain. The ringer pulled twelve times for twelve o'clock, but Big Peter was his own master and ignored the end of the pulls, going on ringing out his deep, sonorous notes which seemed to be part of those who heard, shaking the air about them, seeming to boom through their bodies. Conversations stopped. Strangers looked up in wonderment. The voice of Big Peter can go on for as much as ten minutes until the bell gradually comes to rest, telling its little world that noon is here.

Dr Reiver was approaching the entrance to the Manor from the car-park, his white hair shining in the pale sun. He saw Sophie and raised a hand in greeting, then waited for her by the doorway. Over the door the royal coat of arms gleamed, brightly painted, tremendous against the limestone blocks of the wall.

Without trying to speak through the sound of the bell, they entered the dark hallway, passed the porters' lodge, and went out into the first quadrangle. Here the Friesian calf fashioned in bronze by Sally Arnup stood on its plinth, endearingly domestic, and the tree opposite dared to put forth its buds. All around rose the old buildings.

They climbed the flight of stone steps to the refectory and made their way between the long tables to the serving area at the rear. In this large room early Georgian assemblies had once danced their grave minuets and boisterous country dances. Inside, the voice of the bell was shut out sufficiently to render ordinary speech audible.

'It's cold for salad,' remarked Dr Reiver, 'but I always prefer it at midday.'

'I'm going for a hot meal,' Sophie responded. 'It saves me cooking later.'

They split up, each with a tray, and rejoined at the cash point. The cashier smiled and greeted them. She knew they were both attached to the university and therefore paying the lower tariff.

Settled at an empty table, Reiver made haste to talk as they would probably be joined by other people before long.

'You look a little better,' he remarked, gazing at the demi-lunes of Sophie's upper cheeks as seen through the lower part of her glasses. Two days before they had been red and swollen by weeping, but now the swelling was less and her customary paleness had returned. Her eyelids, though, were as red and swollen as ever.

'I feel just the same,' she answered.

149

'How is the writing?'

'It keeps coming.'

'That is good, I think. I'm looking forward to reading it. We had better talk about the other business when we have more privacy.'

She passed him a sheaf of paper and he laid it at the side of his plate, asked her if she minded, and then began to scan the account of the Yorkist army denied admittance to the city of York.

'There's no denying Edward IV was a consummate politician,' he said at last, placing the pages together as several people approached their table and asked if the other seats were taken. 'We'll talk over coffee. I'll fetch two cups. Do you take sugar? Milk? Shall we take it into the Senior Common Room? I'm a member.'

'I've been meaning to join,' replied Sophie, who had shaken her head and then nodded to indicate that she took milk but no sugar.

'Be my guest today.'

They were soon settled in the long Senior Common Room. An exhibition of paintings hung on the walls and the occasional person wandered in to look at these, but the two managed to find a quiet corner.

'I've found such an exciting thing this morning in the archives,' said Sophie, 'but it's really about the reign of Richard III.'

'Let's cover the gap, first,' said Ralph Reiver. 'Have you written anything about the rest of Edward's reign?'

'I didn't bring it today. It was a bridging section about the next few years. I want to start again properly after Richard came to the throne in 1483.'

'Let's see.' Ralph Reiver threw back his head and scrutinized the ceiling. 'Both sides suffered, didn't they, after the scene you've written. It seems to have been the custom, if you won a battle, to behead the leaders of the other side immediately. Elizabeth Wyville's father and brother were beheaded by the Lancastrians, and Henry VI's and Queen Margaret's son cut down by the Yorkists, after a battle. Now that was completely unnecessary. The boy was running away according to one report. It would have fitted better with the customary behaviour to the royal family to have captured the prince. I remember that when Edward got the throne back he decided it was best to have Henry VI executed, without trial, poor pious soul; no wonder Margaret lost heart after that, with both son and husband murdered. A sad life, one feels. Then a few years later Edward's own brother, the Duke of Clarence, a fickle man who thought to wear the crown himself—it seemed good to be rid of him; he was drowned in wine, so they say.'

'Edward IV was pretty ruthless, actually,' said Sophie.

'It was in that same year, 1478, a few days,

151

not more, after George Duke of Clarence was murdered—or executed, have it how you will—that the king's other brother, Richard Duke of Gloucester, who had been put in charge of the North Countrie, came from London to live in his own manors, his own castle of Middleham in the beauty of Wensleydale with his castle of Sheriff Hutton handy for the town of York.'

'I think he was anxious to get out of the way of his sister-in-law, she was a bit of a bitch. Those she hated were not long for this world. There was the Earl of Desmond...'

They both thought of Edward's close friend who, when asked, had told him it would have been wiser to marry for a good alliance than for love.

'Edward should not have repeated Desmond's words to his queen,' went on Reiver, 'but being besotted with her, and the words not being in malice but as a friend's opinion, he did tell her, or so they say...'

'And in 1467 she had her revenge, via the Earl of Worcester when he became Deputy of Ireland, then indicted Desmond for some imaginary fault and beheaded him.'

'Well, I don't know; you're a historian, Sophie; that story may be part of the later Tudor propaganda. The Earl of Desmond is usually said to have been murdered, I grant you.'

After a while, during which they were both

drinking their coffee, Reiver broke the silence. 'As we've been saying, many men had been beheaded in the wars by both sides, without trial, with never a word said blaming those who ordered it.'

'It was what happened next that was so dreadful,' answered Sophie. 'You remember two of Desmond's small sons were said to have been murdered. That was cruel of Queen Elizabeth if it was true. She had children herself.'

'*If* the story is true. You ought to check on the sources. We have to be realistic about the medieval period,' Ralph reminded her. 'The human animal is cruel. We haven't overcome that, and I don't believe we ever will.' Seeing Sophie's eyes fill with tears, he said hurriedly, 'I'm sorry, my dear.'

'It's all right. I can't help taking general remarks personally at the moment.'

'You promised to tell me what you discovered this morning.'

'I was looking through the city records. There was a man tried for murder, and executed, and he was one of the journeymen at John of Coln's establishment—next to the place we've called Barley Hall, where Mayor Snowshill lived.'

Dr Reiver sat up in his chair and looked as if he was all ears at this. Sophie had spoken so calmly—hadn't she taken it personally? Obviously not. The scholar's abstract passion for facts must be motivating her.

'George would have been so interested. It is rather extraordinary,' she went on.

'Didn't it upset you?'

'No. I realize that's odd. No, instead of making it worse, it somehow made George's death seem more abstract. More like a sequence, less of a strange and isolated tragedy. It made me realize—really realize—how life has gone on for so many centuries in this city, that many things have happened before, perhaps in the same places, perhaps not, birth and marriage and death and hatred and fighting as well as happiness and rejoicing. Every stone must be soaked with happenings, if you look at it that way.'

'And we are only adding to the skein of history?'

'We're living in history, we are history, what happens to us alive today is as real but no more real than what happened to people at other times. That's it. I suppose I found that comforting.'

Not knowing what else to say, Reiver went on, after patting Sophie's hand in a sympathetic way, 'You can't jump to Richard's reign without saying a little about his time from 1478 to Edward's death.'

'Those years were the foundation of his popularity in the north, I feel,' said Sophie.

'Yes. His outstanding characteristic, so different to most people in high places at the time, was loyalty. He was one person Edward IV could always trust. In character he was very different to his brothers. Perhaps it was due to his sickly childhood, when they didn't think they would rear him. He may have had much gentler treatment, without the constant pressure to excel, to be macho. There seems to be no doubt that his love, once given, was given for ever. He loved his brother, his wife, his mother-in-law, his son, his homes, his town of York. He and Anne, you remember, used to stay with the Austin Friars in Lendal, right in the city, and they joined the Guild of Corpus Christi, and supported the Mystery Plays. They obviously loved that spectacle.'

'I don't think he was happy in the south,' Sophie stated dogmatically.

'I'm sure he wasn't. He was almost frightened there, never knowing whom he could trust, surrounded by hidden forces he didn't understand, and people busy feathering their own nests.'

'It seems almost incredible that the main problem of his reign was simply a north/south divide, if that was the case,' Sophie said. 'Can't we ever be free of that? After all, we're a small country, only a few hundred miles from end to end. If we can't regard one another as equals, what hope is there for the world?'

'You may well ask,' said Dr Reiver, looking at his watch. 'I'll have to go, Sophie, and we haven't even mentioned the horrible time you had on Saturday. I did call in at Stonegate this morning, though, to tell Mr Southwell all about it. You know I don't lecture any more but one of the staff is ill and I've been asked to fill in this afternoon. Look, here's my phone number.' He wrote it down on a slip of paper. 'Give me a ring this evening and we'll arrange to meet again. This lunchtime idea is quite good, don't you think so?'

'It's very convenient,' replied Sophie, 'and it's nice having someone to talk to.'

*　　*　　*

Bob Southwell had had a very busy time since his interview with his chief that morning. The media, thank goodness, had been distracted by the discovery of a more newsworthy murder than the one with which he was dealing, and apart from a phone call from the local evening paper, he did not have that worry. There were more than enough things to do, without being sidetracked.

One thing he had done was to slip home at lunchtime to break the news to Linda. Her immediate reaction was to review the state of his wardrobe *vis-à-vis* her laundry programme and declare that he ought to buy a new shirt.

'We've got until Wednesday afternoon,' he reminded her. 'I need to set off then—we've been asked to arrive in time for an evening meal on Wednesday, to settle in ready for the start of the assessments on Thursday morning. You can buy me a shirt, darling. You know my size and what I like. Buy two if you think that's necessary.'

'And socks,' Linda mused.

'Look, if I'm wearing all new clothes I'll feel strange and I need to feel relaxed for this job.'

There was a gleam in his wife's eye and Bob sighed, seeing that he would have to put up with whatever she arranged for him. He kissed her with a little foreboding.

'Don't forget,' were his parting words, 'I need to feel relaxed and comfortable, above all, comfortable.'

Then he dismissed the thoughts of shirts and socks from his mind and began mentally to assess the murder investigation as far as it had gone in four and a half days, ready for his briefing meeting that night. In two days' time he'd have to leave them all on their toes, each man fully aware of progress and alert to anything of significance which occurred in his absence.

CHAPTER NINE

It was towards five o'clock, nearly time for the briefing or debriefing meeting to take place, when Bob was handed a note from Dr Ralph Reiver. He read this with surprise, and kept it by him when he arranged his papers.

'Further to what I said this morning, that I have been placed on the short list for DS,' he began (and there was a murmur from his audience registering approval and support), 'you may have heard on the grapevine that this means I will be away for a couple of days for assessment tests.'

His staff moved into a buoyant, teasing mood when they heard this statement; having become very supportive of Bob since his arrival from Harrogate on promotion to DCI, they felt they knew him well enough to indulge in cries of 'Shame!' and 'Hurrah!'

'Now you can quieten down, you lot. Due to financial stringency, there will be no one to replace me—you will be managing on your own. Mr Smart, I would like you to take the briefings in my absence. Mr Rollo will fill in any other of my duties which need doing and can't be left. You two will work as a team, all right? Good. I can be reached by telephone if absolutely necessary, but will be back on the job by Saturday morning. I'll leave a phone number where you can contact me but I would like you to prove that we have a well-run ship which functions without running to mother every few minutes, yes?'

There was a sort of hum which Bob took to mean assent.

After gazing round the room intently and making eye contact, he went on, 'We have until

Wednesday teatime to make as much progress as possible. It would be ideal if we could solve this by then but at the present rate of progress I don't see that happening, although a couple of things have come up which may possibly be leads. To recap: a great deal of information has been pouring in, and collating and sorting it all, together with what is still arriving, is taking a lot of time. All forensic material has been sent over and we are waiting for reports on that. We are getting results in that most of the workmen on site have already been eliminated from the enquiry. Many of them had good alibis for 9 p.m. to midnight. There are two or three who haven't convinced us yet, but as a group they look increasingly unlikely as suspects. Now I would like to hear progress from each section.'

'We found one man who overheard a quarrel going on that night,' said the head of the team who had been questioning neighbouring businesses and residents. 'He took no notice because, as he said, all sorts go on late at night after the pubs turn out and you can't be taking action every time you hear a quarrel, or a shriek, or what sounds like a fight. As far as he can remember, one man had taken something belonging to another man. And he's fairly sure that it was at half-past eleven because that's when he goes to bed, and he lay listening to the noise. The noise went on until a quarter to twelve, when there was a thump. He heard no more. That's it.'

'Right. That's very exciting, actually. It seems to pin-point the time of death for us,' said Bob. 'We had been assuming, from the medical evidence, that between eleven and twelve must be about right, and if the victim was actually killed at a quarter to twelve that evidence is crucial.'

Bob nodded to the head of another group. 'Can you recap for us on your work last Thursday?'

'We went to search the victim's room, and next day, with the permission of the owner, Mr Caile, went over the rest of the house as well, though not in such detail. The results are in our report, which has been circulated. Briefly, in the victim's room we found fingerprints only of himself, his girlfriend, and his landlord. These last were more numerous than the landlord had suggested to Mr Southwell. He must have given the room a pretty good going over himself. His fingerprints were not localized, but we thought he might have been looking for something of more significance than the victim's address and telephone book. There were very few of the girlfriend's, and those were where one expects visitors' fingerprints to be left.'

'Did you glean anything important from his possessions?' asked Bob. 'Not everyone heard this.'

'He was a fanatically tidy man, but his clothes were a contradiction of that in a sense, because although kept tidily they were all old and worn and looked as if they had been second-hand to start with. Except one suit and shirt, hanging together, which were probably his go-to-meetings outfit. We went through his papers, which were exclusively on his work. His diary was an engagement diary only. It confirmed Miss Beans' outline of their relationship, but the entries were very brief indeed.'

'Money?' asked Bob.

'He seems to have been very frugal. Certainly he didn't spend the whole of his income, or anything like it, although he wasn't earning a lot. It makes a difference, of course, when people don't run a car, eat home-cooked food, don't smoke, hardly drink, don't dress expensively, don't spend much on their social life—no holidays, no theatres or other entertainments. His biggest expense was books.'

'We'd all be rich if we didn't run cars,' a young detective constable put in feelingly.

'He seemed to enjoy life, all the same,' someone else said.

'Apart from enlightening us about his character, there was little really to help with the investigation,' summed up Bob.

'I'm afraid that's correct, sir.'

'The team examined George Followes' room on Thursday and the rest of the house on Friday; on Saturday morning his landlord,

Marius Caile, contacted Sophie Beans and asked her to clear all the victim's possessions from his room that day, alleging that he needed to let the room again quickly to continue his income from the tenancy. While this may be true, it seemed to Dr Reiver, who told me this on the phone, and to me that his behaviour was unnatural and heartless. In fact we had told him that George Followes' parents would be arranging about George's possessions. Miss Beans was very distressed over all this, and although she managed to comply with the request she can hardly move in her flatlet now because of all the victim's belongings.'

Bob paused for breath, and was pleased to know by the silence in the room that everyone was feeling as surprised as he had been.

'Together with this,' he went on, 'we have the report from our team checking on neighbours' memories of the time of the crime, that one lady often heard Followes and Caile quarrelling, contrary to Caile's statement to us that they got on well. The neighbour alleges that they quarrelled at about half-past six on the evening of the murder itself. So Caile moves up into the category of prime suspect, at the moment.'

Bob looked for the glass of water, which he didn't usually need, and had a drink from it.

'Now one other thing has turned up which is rather curious, and again we've been put on to it by Dr Reiver, who is certainly proving useful.

He tells me that Miss Beans, who is researching in the York City Archives, found a reference this morning to a previous murder in much the same spot as this one.'

'Another murder in about the same place?' said DI Rollo.

'Yes. That's strange, isn't it? It was long ago, in the time of Richard III. He's left me a note about it.'

Then Bob remembered something which he had pushed to the back of his mind, because of thinking about the promotion assessments and arrangements for them. Turning to his desk he rummaged in the drawer, and pulled out the photographs taken on the previous day by the woman photographer.

'Have a look at these,' he said, passing the photographs to the nearest member of his staff. 'Pass them round.'

There was complete silence as they were handed round the room. On the wall was an enlargement of a photograph of George Followes' hand. On it someone had drawn lines to show where the pressure marks had been, the ones PC John Clark had drawn in his notebook. Heads were bent to look at the new photos and then lifted to compare the shape shown as a depression in the mortar with the indentations on the palm of the murdered man. It was not until the two photos had made the complete rounds of the people in the room, and been returned to Bob Southwell, that anyone spoke.

'You haven't told us what these photographs are of, sir,' said John Rollo. 'It isn't clear.'

Then Bob had to tell them about noticing the loose brick on his site visit the day before. 'It is only a half-brick actually,' he explained. 'Brickwork is built in what is called bonds, as you probably know, and it is sometimes necessary to use half-bricks in a construction.' He explained about prising it out, and the photographs being taken.

'You haven't told us your opinions, sir,' said Jenny Wren, who had been bursting to speak for several minutes, 'but the indentation you found looks to be the same shape as whatever the victim was clutching so tightly.'

There was a general murmur of agreement. They had all memorised those red marks on the palm, and had all come to the same conclusion.

'It is difficult to judge relative sizes, sir,' said Dave Smart, 'but they've got to be the same object.'

'I took measurements.' Bob waved his pocket notebook. 'Neither the constable nor I could be really accurate, he because he avoided touching the palm, I because my six-inch rule couldn't go inside the cavity. But allowing for that, there's enough correlation for us to be sure it's the same object.'

'So whatever he was holding had at some time been hidden behind this brick in the chimney,' went on Dave Smart.

There was a general murmur of agreement.

'What's more,' and now Bob produced his trump card, 'the interim report received from the forensic laboratory this afternoon says that they found traces of brick and mortar dust on the palm of the murdered man. You remember Mr Smart here bagged the left hand, and we asked them to inspect it with special care.'

Everyone felt that this evidence, although circumstantial, was when put together so strong that surely it would stand up in court.

'So all we need to do is find out what the object was,' said Jenny Wren.

'We need to do a darn sight more than that, but knowing what it was would be another stride forward.'

'It looks as though you've discovered something very important, sir,' Dave Smart said. 'Whatever was hidden must have been valuable. Someone found it, perhaps the victim and perhaps not, and there was a fight over it.'

'That's the possibility. What could it have been, that's what I was hoping one of you might have a guess at.'

'People often used to hide things in chimney stacks,' said John Rollo. 'I mean, I've heard of it before. When they were knocking down an old farmhouse in the Selby area they found an old book and a pen and bottle of ink. The ink was dried up, obviously, but the book had some kind of parish records in. I remember now, it was the village constable's book. It struck a chord, being a policeman's, kind of.'

'Chimney stacks are recognized hiding places, you're right, John. So it's not surprising to find something in a chimney in an old building. So what is it that was hidden in this one?' asked Bob Southwell.

'Was there any forensic evidence in the cavity?' asked Dave Smart.

'It was examined first thing this morning by the forensic scientist, Brian, who you all know. We should have his report soon, and accurate measurements.'

'I said it must have been something valuable,' Dave Smart said after a minute, 'but there are different kinds of value. An archaeologist would value what most people would call a lot of old rubbish. So the object might be something we wouldn't think of as valuable at all. On the other hand, we could be talking about something with a value obvious to anyone, like precious metal.'

Sarah Doughty broke in. 'The murderer will have to be someone with the opportunity to discover something in the chimney.'

'Not necessarily,' John Rollo said. 'It could have been the victim who discovered it, and someone else got to know and tried to take it away.'

'You can ponder the problem overnight,' said Bob Southwell, putting the photos and his notes in his briefcase. 'The bit of brickwork is in a decayed condition,' he went on. 'I imagine they will be patching it up. Most of the chimney stack was in good nick. They aren't likely to demolish the whole thing. If you notice, chimney stacks and gateposts are often left untouched when other things are knocked down.'

'They are restoring Barley Hall to the way it was the century after it was built,' John Rollo said. 'One of the girls in the office was telling me. Round about the time of Richard III. I remembered that because wasn't he a murderer?'

'No, he wasn't,' Sarah Doughty put in hotly. 'You're being taken in by Tudor propaganda.'

Bob Southwell was amused to see that his staff had been momentarily deflected from the matter in hand by the centuries-old dispute. He remembered the battle of Towton and the story he had told Sophie Beans. In York, he thought, the past may be dead but it won't lie down.

'I said earlier that a murder had occurred here in the time of Richard III, not by him,' he put in gently. 'Anyway, I think the chimney stack is much more recent than the Middle Ages. We've got a *modern* crime here, let's get on with that.'

*   *   *

'It was seventeen years after that battle near Towton where I lost the comrade who loved

167

me, that I came north in the Duke of Gloucester's bodyguard, and met a bonny lass in York who made sure that I stayed and wed her,' Sophie had written. 'I was getting past active service, and the good duke gave me a post in his household at Sheriff Hutton castle, so that we could settle down as married people with nothing much to worry us. They had been good years for the country since Edward IV began to reign again in 1471. Beautiful new buildings were going up everywhere, although the king built mainly in the valley of the River Thames. He did not trouble himself to come up north, knowing that our duke and the Earl of Northumberland between them had the area in hand.

After the Duke of Clarence was done away with, Duke Richard treated the north as his sanctuary, so I used to tell my wife. He managed to get his mother-in-law out of prison to live with Anne and himself and their son, and the family were as happy as they could be at Middleham, with no desire to travel south to London and the court except when needs must, and then the duke stayed away no longer than he could help. He was a wise lord, a good and gracious lord, and ruled over a great deal of land, nearly the whole of the North Countrie and the difficult border lands near those raiders the Scots. He made friends with Percy of Northumberland as far as anyone could befriend that cold dumpling, and went out of his way to help the people.

His city of York was beholden to him for many a just dealing. There was the matter of the fish-garths, which caused much distress when the ordinary folk could not catch themselves a bit of fish or row a boat up river for all the enclosures that were made in the water and which were the property of this one or that one, this baron or that monastery. Duke Richard arbitrated over and over again on the matter of fish-garths.

Then King Edward IV died...

Richard knew he would have to go south, for he was named as the young king's Protector, and the Council of the North he had started was to rule while he was away. He was not one of those who decide everything themselves and become tyrants. I can't say I liked seeing him ride off without me in his bodyguard, that time, but he saw what I was feeling and clapped me on the shoulder, telling me I was more use to him where I was. It was an anxious summer, all the same, particularly when I heard he'd written urgently to York saying that all the queen's forces were against him and would they send some armed men immediately to his aid.

Then we heard he'd had to take over as king himself, on account of his nephews turning out to be bastards, and soon he was writing to the York mayor and corporation again saying please would they put on a good welcome because he was coming north with a train of southern nobles and he wanted to show them what Yorkshire hospitality could do.

Well, this was right up their street, of course, and the mayor and aldermen and the twenty-four went in their coloured robes to meet the royal party. There were hangings of arras and rare cloths all along the way, along Micklegate and Coney Street and Stonegate and Lendal and everywhere else for that matter, making the buildings look bright and joyous, and set pieces here and there of speeches and songs and little playlets. There are plenty of folk who act in the Mystery Plays who are only too ready to put on costume and strut and declaim in greeting, any chance they get. There were the city waits playing, and feasts and gifts laid on. It was as good a welcome as any king could desire.

My wife and I had travelled from Sheriff Hutton to the city and settled ourselves in Lendal at the Austin Friars, where Richard liked best to stay, and both of us had been right busy preparing for the arrival, the same as everyone else.

You could tell King Richard III, as he was now, was as pleased as anything, because all of a sudden he decided to have another ceremony here in York, and make his little son, newly come here from Middleham castle, into the Prince of Wales. So he sent in a great hurry for his best clothes from London, with pennants for the soldiers' bills and pikes, and badges for

170

other followers.

After the Minster ceremony was over, King Richard and Queen Anne, with the Prince of Wales between them, walked hand in hand through the city streets, wearing their crowns, only the little prince had a wreath of golden leaves round his head, being lighter and easier than a crown, and all three were smiling as they walked along holding hands, with the people cheering and happy on either side. There was much joy all day, as if we were all one family, celebrating with the ones we loved best.

I was glad, afterwards, that he had had that happy day; it was the happiest in our King Richard's life, that I'm sure of.

The wife and I were there amongst the crowd, enjoying it all, when we saw Alderman William Snowshill, that was mayor once, and the wife went up to him—for she was the daughter of a freeman of the city, and her brother was apprentice goldsmith to the alderman—and she asked him where her brother Dick was, for she'd been hoping to see him.

Then the alderman said Dick had stayed behind in the workshop, because a jewel of the king's had been damaged and brought to the alderman to repair, and Dick was finishing the polishing of it ready to take back, and guarding the workshop generally because you never knew these days, it was best to take care.'

171

*   *   *

Here Sophie had paused in her narrative, and left it for a while, thinking about what came next. It was during this interregnum that she came across the account of the murder unexpectedly, not knowing anything about it earlier. The immediate effect was calming if anything, as she had told Ralph Reiver that Monday lunchtime. It was not until the middle of the night, when she woke sharply from a nightmare, that the reality of it hit her, and emotion swept through her, so that she sat cuddled up near the heater once more in her dressing-gown in the middle of the night, squashed in between several piles of books, her pen racing across the pages in her unformed, sprawling writing.

'The sounds of the day came flowing down the alleyway from Stonegate into the courtyard, so that Margaret Calbeck, servant to Alderman Snowshill, couldn't resist going to the end of the alley to have a look, together with the crowds in the street. She took a bucket with her and upturned it to stand on, so that she could see over folk's heads. This although she'd been told to stay and mind the cooking pots simmering over the banked-down turf fire, and set the tables ready for a feast when the household returned.

The alderman himself was eating with the mayor and the rest, in the second or third room of the king's feast, for there were so many invited that they were taking up the Guildhall and three other large rooms beside. The alderman's lady, though, was returning with the rest of the family and friends who were lodging in the house. They would be feasting in the hall, and singing afterwards round the central hearth, telling stories and generally making merry, servants and all.

Margaret was still standing on her bucket at the entrance to the alleyway, reluctant to go back into the darkness of the kitchens, when her lover came up and caught her in his arms, and she was brazen enough to bend down and kiss him well and truly.

"Has he taken thee back, Tom?" she asked him, looking down into his face.

"Has he hell as like," Tom said. "Yesterday was my last day with the skinflint. I'm a free journeyman, as I told him, and I want a proper day's pay for a decent day's work. I'm as good a silversmith as any John Coln will find in this city and if he won't employ me there's plenty as will."

"Thee won't have any trouble, Tom," and Margaret's voice was full of trust and pride. She got down from the bucket and lifted it to take hold of the handle.

"I'm not going to have to look," Tom said, making to open the pack he had put down at his feet. "Come back a little, Margaret, from the alley end. No, let us into Snowshill's, we'll be private there."

"It mustn't be for long, Tom, they'll be coming back soon enough. I don't want them to catch us, they'd throw me out and then neither of us would have a job."

"Thou always thinks the worst," Tom Richerdson said. He hustled her in through the low door and through the store rooms and offices which were beneath the alderman's great chamber, and stopped under a window.

"Look here." He pulled a pouch from the centre of his pack, and shook out on to the flap of it a dazzle of gold, being several gold rings with a ruby in each, half a dozen golden aglets, each decorated with small jewels, a cross of gold garnished with seven pearls, a golden toothpick, and a flower of gold with a sapphire in the heart of it.

"Where did thee get those from?" Margaret asked in fear.

"From the coffer that stands in my master's parlour, where dost tha think? They're all out seeing the king and queen and Prince of Wales. It was easy."

"But what art thou going to do with them, Tom?"

"What dost tha think? I can get a horse and I'm going far enough so that no one will know either me or these jewels and there I will sell them. Then I'll come and fetch thee, sweetheart, and we'll go to live where nobody knows us. But there's something else I want before I go."

"Oh, Tom! It is all so dangerous!"

"Thee and me have loved one another a long time, haven't we? How dost'ta think we'll get enough money to marry?"

"Oh, Tom!"

"Thee'll do anything for me, so that we can be married, won't tha, Margaret?"

"I will that, Tom."

"Then let me up to where thy master's coffer is, for I know he has a jewel of the king's, and the king has enough, he won't miss it."

"Oh, I don't know, Tom..."

"Come on," he said, and applied the persuasions that he knew from experience she was unable to resist.

In a few minutes, weak as water in his arms, she murmured, "The king's jewel isn't in the coffer, Tom. It's still in the workshop. The young lad, Dick, has been finishing off the repair by polishing it so that it goes back to the king looking brand new again."

"What, that puny youth?"

"Him, yes."

"I'll soon get it off him, watch me. Then I'll have to go quick, or they'll raise the hue and cry. Give me thy kerchief, Margaret, to put round my face, or he'll know me."

From the store place where they were, at the back of the Great Hall, the Swinegate side, a narrow ladder led to the workshops above.

Glancing up as he tied the kerchief round his

face, Tom said to Margaret, "Now go into the kitchen. I'll slip out the back way, thee'll not see me. No one will think thee knowst aught about it. Look, I'll leave my pack here by this door then pick it up as I go. I'll come back with a horse, to take thee away with me, in about a week or ten days. It will take me that long to get rid of the stuff safely. Now into the kitchen, love, don't see anything then thou hast nothing to tell. Say nothing and I'll come for thee soon, ten days at the most. Then we'll be together for ever."

She went, obediently, closing the kitchen door behind her. He crept up the ladder, listening hard. Soon he heard the barely perceptible frisson of the polishing rag moving over the surface of gold, with the finest polishing powder buffing up the shine. He crept up on the slim lad who was sitting at his jeweller's peg in the workbench, intent on his work. There was more light up here than down below, for no jeweller or silversmith can work without light, but for cooking, well, the cook can open the door if he can't see; and for storage, light is better excluded if anything. When a window is open it only brings warmth and flies in with the sun.

Dick was too absorbed in his work to hear the soft footsteps coming up behind him. The first he knew was when a brawny arm came over his shoulder and grabbed the repaired reliquary he was polishing. Dick started up, and could hardly rise on his legs for the chest and shoulders bent over him.

"Tom Richerdson?" he exclaimed. "Is it thee? What are'ta doing here? Gimme the king's jewel, 'tis none of thy master's. What dost'ta think—"

At which he was silenced by a blow to his cheekbone which set his teeth smashing against one another in his head. Slightly built, Dick was no match for Tom, but he struggled to rise to his feet and reached out for the jewel he had been polishing.

A second for thought had made it plain to Tom that if Dick had recognized him in spite of the kerchief, then there was only one thing for it. In the space of a few minutes he pounded the lad and banged his head against the wall until Dick lay as if he would never rise again, with his eyes turned up in his head.

Then Tom stood for a while gazing at the treasure he had in his hand. On one side of the lozenge-shaped reliquary was a great pointed diamond set upon a rose, enamelled white, with an image either side of a man and a woman, who seemed to be meant for Adam and Eve. On the other side was an image of St John Baptist and St Katherine on either side of Our Lady, with seven angels set around, garnished with little diamonds, rubies and pearls. The corner which had been damaged had been repaired so skilfully that Tom could not see where the injury had been, and the polishing had made the whole so bright and fair that it seemed to fill his sight and dazzle him.

He crept over to where Dick lay senseless on the floor and thought that there was little danger now of the lad identifying him, for his breathing was noisy and short, catching and pausing now and then, and his colour was stranger than ever Tom had seen skin before. So he gave Dick a few kicks for good measure and went back down the ladder, just in time for he could hear some of the household returning.

It was then that he realized that if he was caught with the king's jewel on him, they would know he had killed Dick as surely as if they had seen him do the deed. He had to hide that jewel somewhere. Already it gleamed at him knowingly as if it were a live thing. He was in the outer back store room, where the builders had been renewing the wattle and daub infill between the upright beams, and on impulse he knelt down and, near the floor, he pressed the jewel into the wall where the daub was still not set. He worked it into the thickness of the wall right up to the sticks of the wattle and spread the surface of the daub so that the jewel was hidden, then made a mark with his nail so that he could find it again.

He picked up his pack; opening the kitchen door a crack and silently watching Margaret who was stirring the big cauldron, he threw her kerchief inside. Then out the back door and on his way.'

178

Sophie found her brain had stopped working and her eyelids would not stay open. Her writing ceased. She thought now she could sleep. Love! Love betrays. Love cannot be trusted. The scent from George's woolly, which she was sleeping in, came up to reproach her. She went back to bed.

CHAPTER TEN

On the Tuesday morning, early, Sophie Beans wrote out a copy of her notes on the fifteenth-century murder for Dr Reiver, and on her way to the York City Archives after breakfast she popped into King's Manor and left it on his desk. Sometimes she wondered exactly which historical period she was living in, when walking familiarly into this building which in an earlier time and shape had been the meeting place for King Richard III's Council of the North.

When Reiver read the material she had left him, he decided at once to let Bob Southwell have a copy, ran one off on the photocopier, and walked round to Stonegate to leave it at the incident room. By then the morning briefing was long since over, but when Bob Southwell in turn read the notes, he decided to

179

discuss them with his force as soon as possible. Relevant or not, he thought they'd be interested. It was not until the evening debriefing that he had the opportunity.

Before such diversions, there was serious work to do. Marius Caile was to be brought in for questioning after the curious way he had behaved on the Saturday. One of the detective team went along to St Helen's Square, through the stone archway at the side of the Mansion House, and down the slope to the open area in front of the Guildhall. There it was a matter of gaining access to the building by asking to see Caile and showing identification.

After speaking to the detective, a flustered Caile went to apply to his supervisor for leave of absence, then quickly tidied his desk and put on his jacket.

'It's a bit much to be fetched from work like this,' he grumbled as they walked through the tourists in St Helen's Square and made their way up the equally crowded Stonegate.

His companion shrugged. 'You knew we'd want you for more questions,' he answered briefly.

'More questions? You've turned the house over, been into every corner, Mr Southwell and a woman were round questioning me Thursday night, whatever else is there to question me about?'

'Don't ask me, mate,' said the detective, who had taken a dislike to Marius Caile on sight.

He could have told him but that wasn't his job. Fetch him, they'd said, so he'd fetched him. That was it. There was a pile of typing he had to get on with on his desk. He could have done without being sent on an errand like an office boy.

Bob Southwell had decided to interview Marius himself. Where, that was the question. He didn't want to leave the incident room and go to either Fulford police station or the rooms on Colliergate where part of the detective force was still based. But the incident room was full and busy, people, chairs, small tables doing duty as desks, computers and piles of paper, tape recorders and notebooks hiding the serene beauty of proportion which Bob had admired so much.

*   *   *

'We'll go into that temporary architect's office in the rooms over Thomas Gent's Coffee House,' he said at last. 'Jenny, you can sit in. Now what is the procedure at interviews? Recap that to me as we go.'

Marius was being escorted by the detective, both feeling dissatisfied but for different reasons.

Bob stood at the window as Jenny and the detective set up the tape recorder, moved the architect's papers to one end of the table, and rearranged the chairs. From here there was an

181

excellent view of the crane, which Bob had last noticed as he came to work that morning. The top of it had been visible over the rooftops. Now it was working, hoisting one beam of timber after another into the sky and then bringing them down daintily into place. Below in the yard men in orange overalls and hard hats were controlling the movements, shouting to each other, running this way and that. It was curious, standing and watching them through a pane of glass, as if they were in an aquarium, a separate and unreal world.

Once fronting Marius Caile across the table, Bob appeared pleasant and reasonable as he began asking questions. Whatever suspicions he held were hidden, veiled.

'It is very good of you to come in like this, Mr Caile,' he began, thinking once more that Marius reminded him of a parsnip. 'Various things have come up since you and I last met. One of them has aroused our curiosity. On Saturday morning you telephoned your ex-tenant's girlfriend, Miss Beans, and asked her to remove Mr Followes' possessions from your property forthwith.'

'Yes, I did,' replied Marius.

'Doesn't that action strike you as a little precipitate? Under the circumstances, even a little unfeeling?'

'No, it doesn't,' said Marius, startled at the choice of subject. Whatever questions he had expected, it wasn't these.

182

'Could you enlarge on that, Mr Caile?'

Marius felt as though he had been caught on the wrong foot. 'I don't see that it is any business of yours,' he said.

'Oh, but it is, Mr Caile. On a murder enquiry we investigate any unusual circumstances that arise, and your request strikes us as very unusual.'

'I told Sophie at the time. I need the income from letting to help meet my mortgage repayments. I can't afford to have the room standing idle. Before it's let again, it will need redecorating and the carpet cleaning, things like that. That will take time, expenditure not balanced by earnings. That time needs to be as short as possible. So I needed George's—Mr Followes'—stuff out.'

'It didn't occur to you that to make such a sudden demand of Miss Beans was rather unfeeling?'

'No, why should it be unfeeling?'

'When she had lost the person she loved so recently, to be faced with the task of clearing his room?'

Marius shrugged.

Bob felt he was getting nowhere fast and changed the subject.

'Your neighbour, the old lady,' he said, 'tells us that you and Mr Followes were always quarrelling and that she could hear you.'

'That old bitch. You don't believe what she tells you, do you?'

183

'Why not?'

'She'd do anything to get at me.'

'Why should she have that attitude towards you?'

'How would I know?'

'You must have some idea, come now.'

'They get pathological, old women,' muttered Marius.

'There must be some foundation, I would have thought.'

'Well, if you want to know, it's that cat of hers. I won't let it dig up my bit of garden in the back yard. It can dig hers up if it likes, but it isn't going to dig up mine.'

'Difficult to stop cats behaving how they wish, wouldn't you say? What steps did you take to stop the cat digging in your back yard?'

Marius was silent.

'Did you throw things at it, by any chance?'

'You've got to do something,' Marius answered. 'I put stuff down, like pepper, but it didn't seem to do much good.'

'So whenever you saw it in the back yard you threw things at it?'

'Didn't hit it as a rule,' Marius said.

'Did Mr Followes approve of you pelting the cat?'

'Oh, George would have let it in the house and fed it. He was soft on animals.'

'And you weren't. Were you soft on Miss Beans?'

'What do you mean?' Marius sat up as

184

though he had been shot. 'It's got nothing to do with you.'

Bob Southwell sighed. 'I'm trying to get at the truth, Mr Caile, about your relationship with your tenant and his girlfriend. There was something behind your sudden request, your sudden longing to have all trace of the murdered man swept from your premises. The information you gave us before last Saturday seems increasingly suspect. You said you were on good terms, yet your neighbour heard you quarrelling the very evening he was killed. I need an explanation, a proper explanation, of that. You have become very important in our eyes because of your previous lies. You have told us deliberate lies, you have behaved in a way which makes us think there is a great deal more to learn about your relationship with both Mr Followes and Miss Beans.'

Bob Southwell leaned back in his chair for the first time in the interview. He allowed a silence to spread itself, time for Marius to think. But it was still far from the moment when Marius Caile would break and tell the truth.

*   *   *

PC John Clark, who had finished his turn of night duty at the weekend, had been drafted to help with the team of uniform men conducting house-to-house enquiries. He was thrilled to

185

bits to be able to catch up on what had happened in the murder case. After all, he had found the body.

On the Tuesday morning, at the same time as Marius Caile was being brought in for questioning, Clark was sent to interview the neighbours of Eliot Lleyn and Jack Henniker, the neighbours who had been making off in a camper-van when the previous questioning took place. He found the road and the house without too much trouble, and knocked. A man in his late thirties came to the door.

'Dr Wrench?' John Clark asked. 'I'm making a few enquiries. May I come in, please?'

'You're lucky to catch me. I'm usually at school,' said Wrench, who was a teacher of Rural Studies in a comprehensive school. 'I've heard about what's going on. You were here the other day, I take it. Asking about our friends across the road.'

'I have a few questions about Wednesday night.'

'Coffee?'

'Please.'

They sat in the kitchen, a square room with a large window facing the road, gaining an excellent view of the house opposite. PC Clark thought it strange to have a kitchen facing the road; they usually faced the other way, on to a private garden or yard. This kitchen looked as if it was a general living-place. The central

186

table bore a typewriter and piles of papers as well as a vase of wild flowers and the thick hand-thrown pottery mugs in which Dr Wrench prepared the coffee.

'You have a family, I was told,' Clark said, slightly nervous.

'Kids? Oh yeah. Three of the little devils,' the kids' father answered cheerfully. 'Plus the dog and cat. They're somewhere in the garden at the moment, the kids are at school, and my wife is teaching at the Tech. General Studies. You'll have to make do with me.'

'I gather you take off for the seaside or countryside on Friday nights most weekends in your camper-van and come back Sunday nights,' Clark went on, 'so you don't see anything of your neighbours at the weekend.'

'That's true, but you don't want to know about weekends, do you now?' and Wrench sat down with a thump at the table, propped his elbows on it, and slurped his coffee.

'Do you know your neighbours well?'

'Eliot and Jack? Pretty well, yes.'

'Did you see them on Wednesday?'

'I got home about half four. Don't mess about after school if I can help it. They were home about the same time, told me they'd been to an auction sale.'

'Yes, so they told us.'

'If I'd given them half a chance they'd have shown me what they'd bought and I'd have been talking to them—or listening—for an hour, so I didn't linger.'

'Right.'

'Then I saw them going out again later on, about a quarter past seven.'

'Right.'

'That what they told you?' asked Dr Wrench, attacking his coffee again.

'Yes.'

'George was here that night, of course,' cheerful Alan Wrench said. 'You know, George who got himself murdered.'

'Here? Oh? What time was that?' John Clark made another note in his notebook, which he had opened on to the table.

'About half-past nine. I know George pretty well, you see, from when he and Eliot were pally and he was round here a lot. We often used to see him in the old days.'

'What old days were those?' Clark asked.

'Last year, before the big break-up. George used to be round a lot. I expect that's when they gave him a key.'

'Key?'

'Well, he let himself in, that evening. Perhaps he knew where they left it. I saw him and thought he must have gone in to wait for them. About half-past nine, that would be. I was outside getting the van ready for the weekend, so I waved at him and shouted, "Hello, haven't seen you for a bit," I said. He walked over. I told him they'd gone out and what time. He said he'd wait. He went into their house and

188

put the light on and closed the curtains. Then he probably got fed up with waiting, because he went off again in a hurry at about ten.'

'Did he speak to you again?'

'No. Didn't see me. I was in here, at the sink as it happens, but he never looked my way.'

'How did he seem as he went?' asked Clark, who knew that it was important. This sighting was only two hours before he himself had found the man dead at midnight. Well, a couple of minutes after midnight.

'How do you mean, seem?'

'Disappointed ... sluggish, as if he didn't want to leave ... angry at not having located his friends...'

'Friends? They used to be friends, but they're not any more, like I said. He went off walking quickly, head down, annoyed, I would say.'

'And it was some time before your neighbours returned?'

'They rolled up about half ten, quarter to eleven, something like that, in the car. I saw the sweep of the headlights across the curtains as they turned the car to back into their garage.'

'In that case he was gone well before Lleyn and Henniker came back?'

'Oh, yes, ages. I went out and yelled across to them that they'd missed seeing George, and they looked a bit puzzled, then went inside.'

'Thanks very much, Dr Wrench. Is there

189

anything else you can tell me?'

'I don't think so.'

'You've been very helpful, thanks. Thanks for the coffee.'

'Nice to see you.'

Alan Wrench saw the policeman out, pleased to have had a bit of company. He was a sociable man.

PC Clark went off in fine fettle, thinking that he really had something worthwhile to report.

*   *   *

'We'll stop for coffee, I think,' Bob said after the silence had lasted a while. 'Jenny, if you could fetch a supply. Interview suspended for coffee break, ten thirty.'

'I've a lot of written work to catch up on, sir,' said the detective.

'I know you have, Pete, but I'd like you here for the time being.'

It was not until after another hour of questioning, repeating the same queries, going round and round the problems, calmly and patiently at first on Bob Southwell's part, growing more and more fierce and abrupt as time went by, increasingly nervous and moody on Marius Caile's part, that the point was reached where they began to get at the truth.

'How would you like it,' he brought out quickly at last, 'how would you like it if you'd got to live with someone who'd had all the

190

chances you never got? George had it easy. His family were behind him from the word go. Whatever George wanted George got. Direct grant school, university, you name it.'

'And you didn't?' Bob asked quietly.

'Did I hell. No nice privately-owned bungalow for me. I was dragged up on a council estate,' naming the most notorious and problem-ridden in York, 'and my parents cared bugger-all about me. I've had to fight and scrape for everything I've got and everything I'm going to get. But it was him, George, who came begging me for accommodation.'

'Did you resent that? Or did it make you proud of what you'd achieved?'

'I loved him,' said Marius, and put his head down on his arms on the table, and began to weep.

The police personnel were silent. At last Bob said more gently, 'How exactly do you mean that?'

Marius's head came up sharply.

'Not how you're thinking. No wonder you get called the filth. First filthy thought that comes into your mind.'

Bob's firm voice went on, 'No need for remarks of that kind, Mr Caile. Are you telling us that you did not have any homosexual love for Mr Followes?'

'Of course I didn't. What do you think I am?' Tears were rolling down Marius's face.

'Explain to us how you mean the phrase you used, that you loved him.'

'He never talked down to me, he treated me as if I was his brother.'

'But you quarrelled?'

'Yes, well ... He'd had it so easy.'

'You envied his upbringing and opportunities?'

'I'm not bloody perfect. Yes, I was jealous. Then he got Sophie. As if he didn't have enough already, he had to find Sophie.'

'Do you mean that Sophie came between you? Is that what you mean?'

'I can't bear it.' Marius's head went down on his arms again. 'I couldn't bear it.' His voice came muffled by the sleeves into which his face was pressed.

'What couldn't you bear, Mr Caile?'

'Instead of us talking together he'd be in his own room with her. She used to sit on his bed and read while he worked on the computer. She'd come into the kitchen and make a drink for both of them. Oh, she'd ask if I wanted one too, but I always said no. Sometimes she'd eat with us. Sometimes she stayed the night. And I sleep in the room above. I'd know they were together down there.'

'Didn't you tell him you would prefer it if she didn't stop the night?'

'Yes. We quarrelled about that, if you want to know. I expect that was what the old bitch next door heard. I told him I didn't want goings-on under my roof. Only I put it a bit plainer than that,' said Marius, glancing at Jenny.

'How did you feel about Miss Beans? Did you like her?'

'Oh, I liked her all right,' said Marius.

'You liked her very much?'

'Yes, I liked her very much.'

'Would it be putting it too strongly to say that you loved both of them, in different ways?'

'I suppose I did,' the younger man muttered.

'You were excluded? I'm sure they didn't mean to be unkind. Young people in love tend not to realize the effect their behaviour is having on others.'

Marius could say nothing for his sobs, muffled only by the sleeves of his shirt. Bob regarded the crown of the young man's head, which was all he could see of him. Even parsnips, he thought, have hearts that can break. And when hearts are breaking, brutal behaviour can be the result.

They let him recover his composure, or some of it.

'Did you murder your tenant, Mr Caile?'

'How can you say that!'

'I must ask the question.'

'No, I didn't murder him.'

'Did you see him again that evening, after six o'clock when he left the house to go to Miss Beans's flat?'

'No, I didn't see him again.'

'Why did you ask Miss Beans to remove his things at such short notice in that very unfeeling way?'

'Unfeeling! Unfeeling! Haven't you any idea?'

'Why did you behave in that way, Mr Caile?'

'I couldn't stand it. The way he'd died. His things about the house. I couldn't stand seeing her mourning for him. I couldn't stand any of it. I had to get rid of everything. Everything that reminded me. I never wanted to see her again. I couldn't bear it, not any of it.'

'Interview concluded,' Bob said to the tape recorder.

They stood up, the detective and the detective superintendent and the police constable. They stood erect and looked at the sobbing man.

'Jenny,' said Bob, 'ring his office and tell them he isn't feeling well and has gone home. Pete, fetch some tea, will you?'

Bob turned his back and looked down through the window into the yard, and noticed how many beams they had brought over, and watched the carpenters fitting one into position. The work with the crane would last three weeks, and for the whole of that time the ordinary public were to be barred from the courtyard of Barley Hall, and the through alleyway was closed to them. Bob stood at the window for ten minutes, until Pete returned with beakers of hot tea.

194

'Drink this,' Pete said with a rough kind of friendliness to Marius Caile, putting a beaker of tea down in front of him. Then he passed one to Bob and took one himself. Jenny had gone to telephone and not reappeared.

Half an hour after the conclusion of the interview, Bob sent Marius Caile home, driven in a police car by Jenny Wren.

*   *   *

The evening case meeting was at five.

The policemen came in from Stonegate and then through a door in the wall and up the stairs. Doing this they couldn't see what was going on in Coffee Yard, but all the police staff on the case had become interested in the progress of the building work, and snatched a minute or two to watch whenever they could, in the yard itself.

Bob Southwell, after brief introductory remarks, said, 'Let's have any reports of today's results.'

PC John Clark could hardly listen to the other reports. He was longing to talk about his results. He didn't exactly keep reminding everyone that he'd found the body, but his own consciousness of it gave him a glow of interest which other members of the force could not help noticing. Now, at last, he took his turn in reporting progress.

'I was sent to interview the family who were

on holiday at the weekend—neighbours of Eliot Lleyn and Jack Henniker at Heslington,' he began. 'Name of Wrench...'

It was a good feeling, adding something concrete to the progress, a later sighting of the victim, a revelation of previous friendship warmer than had so far been revealed to them.

'Very interesting,' Bob Southwell said thoughtfully when PC Clark had finished. 'That throws new light, John.'

Clark's was the last report; after discussion of the main thrust of the next day's enquiries, Southwell was able to end the meeting with a different note.

'Do you remember,' he began, 'that I told you Miss Beans had found the record of an earlier murder on this site? Listen to this. There was a hearing before the mayor, nine of the twelve (I think they were the aldermen) and eight of the twenty-four. They were ordinary council members I suppose. Now for the quote.

'"At which day Margaret Calbeck, late servant to Alderman William Snowshill, came in her proper person, and was there examined of the taking of the goods of John de Cologne, goldsmith of this city, and of a jewel of the King's. She said and confessed that Tom Richerdson, journeyman, came unto her at her master's house and communed with her of the old love betwixt them, and so promised to wed her, and he had certain jewels, and said that if she was in favour he would take also the jewel

196

belonging to our gracious lord King Richard which was at her master's house in the coffer, and he should take the jewel forth, and soon after purvey him of a horse and shortly go to a place where no man should know him. Then she said that the jewel was not in the coffer but in the workshop where the apprentice was, and she saw the said Thomas no more that day. Later it was found that the apprentice was nigh unto death and the jewel was gone. Three days later this Tom Richerdson came to a house in Larethorp where the said Margaret was, and she told him the apprentice was dead. Then he said he would come to fetch her on the Sunday next following, and he came not, but sent to tell her he had gone to Ripon to his father and mother, and since that time she has seen him not.'''

'Things don't change much, do they?' commented DI Smart when Southwell looked up from the piece of paper in his hand and waited for their reaction. 'Left in the lurch, and intent on revenge.'

'That's sexist, Dave Smart,' exclaimed Sarah Doughty in a low voice she hoped Bob Southwell wouldn't hear.

'But the real nub is here, in the description of the jewel, and Dr Reiver—or rather Sophie Beans—has given us the original wording for that too.' Then Southwell read aloud, '"A jewel of our lord King's like a lozenge, the bodie of golde engraved on one side with Our

197

Lady holding her son attended by two saints, within a border of angels, garnished with sparkes of diamondes, rubies and pearl. The other side having thereon a white rose, with a great pointed diamonde at its heart, between the figures of Adam and Eve.'"

Bob turned silently to the place on the wall where the photograph of the palm of George Followes' hand was pinned, superimposed by the lines of John Clark's diagram, showing the indentations where he had clasped something tightly and the edges had dug into his flesh.

'At yesterday's briefing we all agreed that it looks as though whatever had been hidden in the chimney might be what the murdered man had been holding. Laugh if you like,' Bob said, 'but doesn't it occur to you that the object could have been a jewel as described? Where we usually mean one stone by the word "jewel", they meant the whole thing. It was possibly a pendant.'

There was no doubt that a large, thick, lozenge-shaped gold pendant with a 'great pointed diamonde' projecting on one side could well have made the marks. The longer the group of policemen and women thought about it, the more convinced they became.

'It doesn't make sense, though, sir,' said Sarah Doughty. 'The only way our victim could have got hold of this old pendant, was if someone found it during demolition of the building. We've been told that nothing of value, nothing even unusual was found. This man Tom Richerdson must have got away with the jewel and had it melted down or sold it to someone who melted it down. Otherwise it would have been found long ago.'

'It's very strange,' murmured Jenny Wren.

'I'm not saying these marks must have been this ancient pendant,' said Bob. 'All I'm saying is that if it was the right size, it could have caused them. Perhaps someone else had read these old records before Sophie Beans did, and had a replica made. Have you thought about that possibility?'

DI John Rollo said, 'But the recess behind the brick, sir, which does look like the pattern of marks PC Clark drew, was in a later bit of building. Didn't you ask someone to check the date of the chimney brickwork with the girls in the Trust office upstairs?'

'Yes. Actually I checked myself. The brickwork is believed to be of the end of the sixteenth century, or even early seventeenth. A long while after the murder in the reign of Richard III, which can be dated pretty exactly to the fifteenth century, 1483 to 1485. In the time of Richard III they didn't have chimney stacks, although maybe the biggest and flashiest castles or royal palaces had started to use them. Here in York, they were still using central hearths in the main room, with a little arrangement in the roof for the smoke to find its way out.'

Jenny Wren put the general feeling into words. 'It's all so ... so ... so far-fetched, sir.'

'So different to everyday life,' her friend Sarah backed her up.

'This whole case is different to everyday life.'

'Yes, sir, but ... Richard III ... and jewels from such a long time ago ...'

'There's one in the Yorkshire Museum,' Bob responded tartly, 'from very much this period, found at Middleham castle fairly recently, and Middleham castle is where Richard III was brought up and he lived there again later in his life.'

'That jewel's diamond-shaped as well,' said someone.

'This, if I'm right, had the corners chamfered.'

'Could be a replica,' came another voice, ready to be convinced.

There was another long silence as the group took all this in.

Bob found himself rather daunted by the unusual quiet. Police personnel more commonly reacted in an outspoken and forthright way.

'What's up with you all?' he asked at last. 'Cat got your tongues?'

'There was an appeal for the museum to buy that jewel they have, it's a reliquary actually,' Sarah Doughty said, 'and if I remember rightly, it cost two and a half million pounds.'

A few people drew in their breath.

That would certainly provide a good motive for murder.

CHAPTER ELEVEN

'I am old. Old and tired, and not willing to live much longer in the world. When we lost King Richard the heart went out of me. It seemed as if it was all downhill, after that day, that incomparable day when he and Queen Anne and their son walked hand in hand crowned with gold, smiling at their people, all sharing in joy, through the streets of York.

The boy had always been weakly. Richard had been weakly as a child, so he deceived himself that the boy would be all right and would grow up as he himself had grown, given the peace and pure air of Wensleydale. But the boy faded away and died. The parents were beside themselves with grief, for they never had but the one ewe lamb.

King Richard had to bestir him, of course, but the queen could sit quiet and grieve. Anyone could have told Richard that Warwick's daughters had decline in the blood, both the sisters were so white and honey-pale, neither of them with the common strength of low-born lasses. But he'd loved her as a child and love was lifelong, for him there was no other.

When she died too, that was the end. He was

alone in the South Countrie, for all he summoned friends from the north and gave them good positions. He pressed on, for if you are a king there is always duty. He did his best to right some of the wrongs his brother had done; there was King Henry VI for a start, who had been done to death regardless; Richard had his body moved from Chertsey to Windsor and interred near Edward, his murderer.

And then there were the bastard princes. Elizabeth Woodville knew it was not Richard's fault, whatever happened to them, for the laws of inheritance had been so abused by Edward that the nobles of England wanted their downfall.

So Richard went on, granting pensions to widows, chivalrous as ever to women, even the Woodvilles and even that Lady Stanley, and if he'd had any sense he should have cut off her head. But Jane Shore, Edward's mistress, he made her take the ordained punishment for adulterers and walk the streets barefoot wrapped only in a sheet, for if it was justice for the common women of England then it must be justice too for her—one law alike for rich and poor. Yet he bore no lasting grudge, once she had performed her penance.

He was dead against unfaithfulness, our Richard, and though he'd had a bastard child himself in his young days before he was wed, the young man got no outstanding preferment. The heir as Richard saw it was the legitimate eldest son of his sister Elizabeth who married the Duke of Suffolk, and so he had him proclaimed.'

* * *

Sophie Beans lifted her head from the paper on which she was dashing down the story she was writing, the story of one Welsh archer. She felt drained, as though there was no more writing in her that day, yet she wanted to finish. The part left to tell was the end, the sad end. She thought she would go out and walk a bit in the strong, cold March wind which was blowing the trees she could see from her window. Today she was not going into town and working. She had the desire to be alone and write and was free to indulge it; Dr Reiver had urged her to write when she felt the need.

She packed a cheese sandwich and wrapped herself up in George's jumper and her anorak and went out. It was the best thing she could have done. The cold rushing air revived her. As she walked out of the city by the river, the water in its wide channel seemed a companion, birds circling over it, ducks swimming on it. When she found a riverside seat and stopped to eat her sandwich the birds spotted her and came crowding to see if she would throw bread to them. She watched the mud-coloured Ouse as it flowed past on its way to the sea and threw bits of crust on to its surface for the ducks.

It was no use, Sophie thought, she had to nerve herself to write the end. Then the curious compulsion which had filled her would be sated and the thought of those long-ago people lifted from her mind. Turning to return to her flatlet, she wondered what would take its place.

* * *

'Then at last came the usurper, Henry Tudor Earl of Richmond, and it became plain that our good Richard had no real interest left in living. He sent for help to York, but before our men could reach him he'd followed his father's example, refusing to wait for support but riding out single-handed if necessary against his foes. Did he think he could reach that usurper and cut him down? No chance of that, for Henry cowered behind the battle and waited in safety for the outcome. With his truest friends riding with him and then dying all round him Richard pressed on, ever nearer to that skulking coward, and died a brave death at the last, fighting against more men than even he could vanquish. All those years of boyhood when he trained his frail frame to acquire strength, that strong right arm and well-muscled shoulder that had cost him so many tears of weariness and hours of effort so that he became a better and stronger fighter than men born big and hearty, all gone under that rain of blows by the traitors who supported the Tudor.

It was as if a pall of blackness settled over the North Countrie, and I, who had known him and followed him so long—I felt it more, maybe, than others, as if it was the death blow for me too.

My wife, bless her, does her best to comfort me, though she had her own troubles in the murder of her brother. Even watching that Tom Richerdson swing on Tyburn tree did not cure that sorrow for her. Well, it is a new time, a new order, the old order passeth, and it was plain by the first letters the Lord Mayor received from the usurper that this time it was an iron fist without a velvet glove. No more will York ask its sovereign to arbitrate in local wrangles, and if we resist his demands to put his place-men in power in our city it will be the most that we can do.

We're used to our rulers heading men, for that is the power of kings and the right and proper end of the lives of their enemies, but none will head as many as this Tudor, I can see that, and unimportant though I am, he has made an end of me too, that I do believe.'

*   *   *

Sophie stared around, dazed, blinking her eyes. There, it was finished. She felt purged, lightened, almost as if she would float away, yet at the same time tired. The present with all its problems came rushing back. Round her feet were heaped George's notebooks and files. Crowding her room were his desk and computer. By the wall were his books.

She unexpectedly felt the wish for company, for seeing someone outside her conflict, like Dr Reiver. If he were free this afternoon it would be good to take another walk in the clean wind, talking about history.

* * *

It was the day Bob Southwell was to go for the two days of assessments. He had been busy all morning clearing his desk of outstanding work Dave Smart and John Rollo might not be able to deal with. That had occupied him very satisfactorily; he hadn't once thought about what was coming. But when he was satisfied he was leaving things in a good state, restlessness took him home for a lunch break.

'I've bought you new socks,' said Linda. 'They're exactly the same as your last lot so you shouldn't feel too new in those. And I bought three new shirts while I was at it, but they're the same make and size as your usual too. Have a look at them.' She produced the boxes.

Bob peered at the labels inside the collars. 'They look all right,' he said.

'I'll take all the pins out and pack them except the one you'll be wearing.'

They were in the kitchen, and Bob was

drying the few pots they'd used, which Linda had washed.

'Now, I want you to do something for me,' she stated firmly. 'I've spent all morning—'

'All right, don't go on. What is it?'

'There's an auction sale in town tomorrow and the view day is today. I'd like you to drop me off for it. In fact, what I'd really like is for you to come in with me and have a look round. We hardly ever go doing ordinary things together and this is a new experience. I shall feel a bit shy, walking in on my own.'

Bob looked sceptical. He thought Linda would walk to the top of Everest if she took it into her head that she wanted to. What maggot was this that had got into her?

'But you don't like old things,' he pointed out. 'You always say things people buy at sales are tat and you wouldn't have them in the house. Why on earth do you want to go to an auction sale?'

Linda smiled at him. It was one of those devastating smiles designed to help get her own way.

'It's for the school play Sue's in,' she explained. 'The teacher's asked me to help provide her costume. They want old-fashioned things and there are some suitable ones in this sale. They'll need adapting, of course, but I can do that. Then when the play's over the school can have them. No, I wouldn't want them permanently cluttering up the house.'

She produced a catalogue and said, 'We'll have to go along this afternoon. The lot numbers are marked. I'm to buy them for other children as well if I can. There are dresses and coats and hats from the sixties and seventies.'

Bob had finished drying the pots and he'd been about to put his jacket on and dash back to work.

'Look, Lin, I'm the Senior Investigating Officer on a murder case. I can't take time off to view auction sales. What's more, historic costume is going to cost the earth—who's paying for it?'

'They're hardly historic and they won't cost the earth. They're all items in good supply and rather plain, nothing special, and anyway the PTA are paying for it, and you were working last night until midnight on the wretched case.'

It was true that he needed an hour or two off, he felt that himself, and he had only been at home a short time for a quick lunch, and would be whizzing away again at teatime for two whole days.

'Where?' asked Bob.

'St Olave's parish hall.'

'Oh well, could be worse. I'll bring you back as soon as we've had a look, if it's a quick look.'

*   *   *

Almery was a narrow lane which joined Marygate about a third of the way up from the bottom. Since the Southwells came to York there had been some new building there; a row of pleasant little terrace houses had been demolished and a new row of little terrace houses built in their place. It was difficult to see the point of the exercise; the new ones were not as pleasant to look at as the old ones, but no doubt they had more plumbing and power points.

St Olave's parish hall was a one-storey building rising sheer from the lane, nearly opposite a workshop which had once been a useful plumber and glazier's but was now something more 'with-it'. From the hall down the lane and across into the Museum Gardens, a gang of horned devils had once capered and shouted, frightening old ladies and causing general disruption, while the quieter members of a medieval crowd had passed along without exciting comment, every day for three weeks.

The hall was full when they arrived there. The goods for sale filled the large room and overflowed into the smaller one. The items of costume were in the smaller and more claustrophobic room; in two minutes flat Bob was saying to Linda that he would wait for her in the larger place. There he found a comfortable chair in one of the rows set out for use the following day, and relaxed. A few other people were also taking advantage of the chairs.

Bob's thoughts went back to the last time he

had been in this hall. Then it had also been because of costumes, the new ones made for the Mystery Plays, and the place had looked completely different. It was near that wall, he remembered, that he had found the row of devils' outfits, red and black, each with its great horned helmet on the floor below it.

The reverie was disturbed by an oldish man, who came and sat in the next chair. 'Good to rest the feet,' he remarked to Bob.

'Yes, yes, it is.'

'Are you coming to the sale tomorrow?' the older man asked.

'I doubt it.' Bob smiled. 'My wife probably is. Are you?'

'No, I think not. I may leave a bid or two. There is nothing worth my staying in York for.'

Bob looked at him more closely. He was a short, stocky man in a brown velvet jacket, cream shirt, brown striped tie, and fawn slacks. As the old, large-pored skin of his face bore a faded tan, the effect was of overall brownness. His face was strongly featured, alert, bright-eyed, with a prominent rather short nose, thick folds of skin from nose to mouth and across his forehead, and he had scanty but coarse hair cut close and brushed neatly.

'I know very little about antiques,' Bob volunteered. 'Wouldn't know where to start. I suppose in any sale there are only a few plums.'

The older man gave him a sharp glance. 'Not

many worthwhile pieces, as a rule,' he agreed. 'Specialist sales are a different matter. If you were interested in silver, now, there would be a couple of items here which might tempt you.'

Bob laughed. 'My wife is buying costumes for a school play,' he said, 'and our budget doesn't run to silver at the present. One day, it might be interesting. As a matter of fact, silver is one field I wouldn't mind being involved with.'

'Old pieces develop a lovely lustre, a patina,' replied the man.

At that moment Bob saw someone he knew slightly. Jean Howard was one of York's antique dealers. Her specialist knowledge had been useful to him more than once, and she seemed to find pleasure in helping the police. She was a very slim, middle-aged woman not much over five feet in height, wearing plain dark clothes and with her black hair sleeked back over her head. He realized she had been there for some time, moving intently to and fro up and down the long tables which held a variety of items for sale. Because he had been thinking of other things he had seen her without registering the fact, but when he realized and looked straight at her she seemed to feel his glance and walked over towards the chairs.

'Fancy seeing you here,' she said.

'I am not surprised to see you,' he countered. Looking past him, she smiled at the man in brown. 'Nothing for you here, is there, Henry?' she asked.

He lifted both hands in a theatrical gesture.

'I'm leaving a couple of bids,' he said in a tone of profound indifference.

She threw her head back and laughed.

'My dear,' she went on, talking to the man in brown, 'if you're staying in York do come for supper tonight.'

'Jean, there's nothing I would like better, if only I were staying, but alas, I am not.'

'Well,' and she went on looking at him with a kind of suppressed twinkle, 'when you do visit the capital of the North Countrie why do you haste away so soon?'

'Business.' He sounded deprecating. 'But your business may bring you to the metropolis, and I promise you lunch if you call.'

'Not afternoon tea on this occasion?'

'That too if you would like it.'

During this exchange he had risen and was obviously ready to go. Turning to Bob he said, 'Charmed to meet you. I will leave you to the tender mercies of this mutual acquaintance of ours,' and to Jean, he said, '*A bientôt.*'

As he turned away she called out to him, 'Mind you scald your jugs!'

He did not look round, but raised a hand in a gesture which humorously acknowledged her remark.

As soon as the man was, Bob thought, out of earshot, he turned to Jean and said, 'Now tell me, what on earth was all that about?'

She laughed again. Meeting the man in brown seemed to have filled her with mirth. Her thin-lipped laughing mouth made a wide scarlet gash across her face, showing the shine of teeth.

'He's one of the top dealers in the country,' she said. 'I'd like very much to know why he is here. It has to be something extra special. That stuff about leaving bids—there's nothing here today he'd cross the road for. The sales in this hall are excellent, but this one is more for collectors of fabrics, costume, books, bric-à-brac. As I heard him saying to you as I came up, there's some good silver. All nice stuff, but not his interest, no way.'

'Explain his interests more to me,' Bob asked.

She shrugged and thought before answering.

'Things have to be very special. Rare and of first-class quality and worth a lot of money. Of international interest. I've known him buy antiquities; items with royal connections if well authenticated; jewels, particularly antique Roman or Greek or medieval European; rare and exquisite furniture; Persian carpets of the palace type and superb condition; paintings, but they'd have to be Vermeers or Van Goghs...'

'That was an odd remark you made to him as he went, "Scald your jugs"?'

Jean laughed again, and went on chuckling

for a while before saying, 'It's a private joke really, between us. He often asks me for afternoon tea when I'm in London. He takes it with lemon but I like milk. One day the milk was off. He told me it was fresh, but when I examined the jug, it hadn't been washed out properly. There were some little joins, too, which were harbouring solid sour traces of old milk, which had tainted the new ... it's trivial but I've teased him about it ever since and told him to scald his jugs with boiling water.'

It was at that point in the conversation that Linda appeared from the smaller room and indicated that she had seen all she needed to. After chatting for a minute with Jean, she and Bob left the hall.

'I must go, darling,' Bob said as he stopped the car at their own gate, and bent sideways to kiss her.

'Try to be in good time tonight.'

'I'll have to be early.'

*   *   *

When Bob reached the incident room, he asked for Dave Smart.

'How is the checking of people's whereabouts going, Dave? The workmen on site and the others who knew the victim?'

'I think we've got hold of most of the neighbours and everyone now, boss, but there is a bit more checking out of alibis to do. If you add up all the bods we've had to confirm movements of, it's quite a few.'

'Look, I'm going to add to your burdens. I want you to ask all the neighbours—go back over those who've already been questioned—if they've seen a short stocky man dressed in a brown velvet jacket and fawn slacks anywhere near where our victim contacts live. Probably travelling by taxi, the taxi might have waited around for him and been noticed. Look, I'll write a description and you can check with the taxi drivers too, Dave. There might be time for me to do a photofit. Then ask all our contacts themselves if they have seen such a man. Be prepared for lies, there.'

'When is this for, boss? When might they have seen him?'

'Yesterday or this morning, I would guess.'

'New information?' asked Dave.

'Call it a hunch, Dave. I'll explain later. There's been one or two things set me thinking but I'm probably completely wrong. Just get me the info.'

'Surely will, boss.'

*　　*　　*

Bob knocked off at half-past four and went home, after a last quick word with Rollo and Smart. Linda had packed for him and his suitcase stood in the hall. He put his briefcase beside it.

'I'll go up for a bath, love,' he said.

The rest of the family were in the kitchen, eating their tea round the white formica table, and Susan and Paul looked up at him wordlessly, with their mouths full and munching. Linda swallowed quickly and came out to him in the hallway.

'How long have you got?' she asked.

He glanced at his watch. 'An hour at most,' he said. 'They want us there for the meal at eight and I'm not rushing down. If I leave at six I should have plenty of time.'

'Do you want anything to eat before you go?'

He looked dog tired and Linda refrained from saying so.

'I caught a sandwich as it was passing around four o'clock.'

'Let's have a quiet half-hour together before you set off,' she suggested.

'Relax by the fire? I wouldn't mind, as long as I don't get too relaxed and not go at all.'

'I'll make you a strong coffee and you can drink it in your armchair. I'll see you set off in time.'

On their bed his clean clothes lay waiting to be put on after his bath. He didn't usually get coddled like this, and tonight was glad of it.

When the children had eaten tea they shouted, 'Bye-bye, Dad!' through the bathroom door and then dashed off to a friend's house, where they had been invited to

216

see his new computer game. Susan wasn't really interested in such games, but there was a doll's house which belonged to their friend's mother, and that she was interested in; she knew she'd be allowed to play with it if she was very careful.

Linda kept herself busy clearing up and making the sitting-room extra welcoming. When Bob appeared, refreshed and wearing different clothes, he settled down comfortably in his favourite chair and she sat on the white fluffy hearthrug and gazed into the artificial flames of the gas fire. Music was playing gently.

'Mmmm,' he said, looking down at her. 'Have we got time for...'

'We daren't risk you setting off late.'

'I suppose you're right.'

About ten minutes later he said drowsily, 'Jean Howard made an odd remark today to a man I was talking to, an antique dealer she knows. He was going and she called out to him, "Scald your jugs!" and told me afterwards that he had once given her milk in her tea from a jug which hadn't been properly washed and the sour traces had turned the new milk.'

'Possible, I should think,' Linda murmured in the direction of the fire. 'Small milk jugs can be the dickens—you think you've got them clean and they're not. Some of them have sort of little crevices in the joint of the metal near the spout.'

'I can see that it's possible but I think there

was a double meaning there somewhere.'

'*Double entendre*? You mean they go to bed together?'

'They were pally, not romantic. No, it's not that.'

'If they were talking of something else … a tainted vessel would taint the goods, is that it?' and Linda gave Bob what he called her 'old-fashioned' look, like a knowing child.

'Could be.' They looked at one another and both felt as though they were thinking the same thoughts, vague, formless but getting somewhere.

'It's time you had that coffee.' Linda got up and went into the kitchen. 'Any more relaxed and you'll be asleep.'

*   *   *

DI Rollo stayed in the incident room after that night's debriefing. He stood by the desk Bob Southwell had been using and looked at the papers there.

'What's this, Dave?' He held up the photofit Bob had managed to organize before leaving.

'That's the chap we have to ask about tomorrow. You heard me telling the teams there was to be another round of questions.'

Rollo read the description Bob had carefully worked out.

'I've seen this man,' he said flatly.

'You have? When? Where?'

'Here. In Coffee Yard. Yesterday.'

'You're having me on.'

'No, I'm not. He's distinctive. He was talking to one of the joiners. That dark one, curly hair, wears a navy shirt and jacket. Richard, I think he's called. Rick, they call him here. In fact he seemed to be getting Rick to show him something in the building, they went up a ladder. I didn't notice them after that, got called on to something else.'

'Magic,' said Dave Smart. 'And Richard is the only one who can't prove where he was.'

CHAPTER TWELVE

On the Thursday morning, as the teams of police set out once more to go the rounds with a questionnaire, this time about the brown-jacketed man, Sophie was making coffee in her flatlet for Dr Ralph Reiver.

He was appalled at the clutter in the place. Although he had found a chair to sit on, stretching out his long legs was impossible.

'You can't put up with this for long, my dear,' he said.

'I will be all right. Sorting everything out mustn't be rushed. It's a sacred trust. George's parents want me to see if there's anything of his which could be published, as a memorial to him.'

'A very good idea. That should be done. No better memorial to a scholar.'

He looked at her and noticed that she was wearing a scruffy, grubby old jumper too long for her, which looked like a man's. Nice girl, Sophie, but he liked to see young women take a pride in their appearance.

'So how are you?'

'I've finished that bit of writing I was doing.' Sophie avoided his question.

'I'd like to read it, if I may.'

She gave him a cup of coffee and the manuscript, then sat quietly drinking her own and looking through one of George's files.

'Hmmm,' he said, when at last he put her notebook back on the table under the window. 'You've come down very much on the side of Richard III. Are you a subscriber to the theory that makes him out to be a saint?'

'No, he could be violent and unfair the same as any other Plantagenet.'

'Any other medieval king? The Plantagenets didn't have a monopoly of brutality and injustice,' said Dr Reiver.

'Dr Reiver—' began Sophie.

'Ralph, please,' he interrupted.

'Ralph, then—do you feel like a walk this morning? It's not too bad outside at all. We could walk along the tow path by the river, past St Peter's playing fields towards Clifton. The scenery there always reminds me of a Dutch painting, flat greenness, water, and willows.'

'Yes, I would enjoy that.'

Sophie collected some old bread for the ducks.

As they walked down to the river bank the discussion was starting already.

'Sophie, you really can't condone the way Richard III behaved to Hastings. Surely he can't be forgiven that summary execution. And as for getting his mother-in-law out of prison, many historians say he only wanted to lay his hands on her property. Now ...'

They walked out from the city, one tall, massive-shouldered male figure, stooping slightly, silver-white hair floating, and nearby the short, dumpy figure of a girl, both with hands deep in pockets, intent on an argument which will last as long as there are people who think Richard III was good and people who think he was evil, and others who are historians and know that nothing is ever truly black and white.

*   *   *

John Rollo and Dave Smart had decided one of them had better be in the incident room or elsewhere on site at all times, during Bob Southwell's two-day absence. Otherwise they might have gone off to the pub together at lunchtime, and had a natter. As it was, they went up into the temporary architect's office, where the architect was busy with his papers.

221

'Oh, all right,' he said when they asked if they might use it. 'I did tell Mr Southwell he was welcome, when it was free. I've finished here anyway for today. What have you been using it for?'

'Interviewing witnesses,' Dave Smart explained. 'The incident room is hardly suitable. We've only taken advantage of your offer for brief periods. All that's involved is using the chairs and table and bringing the tape recorder up and using your plug. I don't suppose it takes much electricity.'

'That's all right.' The architect was magnanimous. 'I was grateful for your co-operation about the crane. What do you think to it now it's in operation?'

'Great,' said John Rollo. 'We all watch it when we get the chance.'

'So you're wanting to interview someone now?'

'We will be, presently. We're making enquiries about a man in a brown velvet jacket who was seen on site yesterday.' Dave Smart produced the photofit picture.

The architect shook his head.

'Never seen him,' he said, 'but I wasn't on site yesterday anyway.'

When he had gone the two detectives were silent for a while, looking out of the window and watching what was going on.

'It would be great if we could clear this case up while the DCI's away,' said Rollo.

'Yep.'

'What about this carpenter, Rick?'

'Better have him in. He has to explain his whereabouts on the night of the murder. He might as well tell us what that man was doing on site while he's at it.'

'You interview him if you like,' said Rollo.

'Right.'

'I'll get back to the incident room and check how the paperwork's going.'

*　　　*　　　*

The other detective present at the interview was James Jester, who had been on night call, then done double shifts while the scene of crime team were working against time, and now was back on his normal schedule. He still felt sleepy now and then after all the hours he had put in the previous week, but it had been worth it. He dogsbodied happily this morning for Dave Smart, checking the tape recorder, moving the architect's papers carefully to one end of the long table, placing the chairs.

The carpenter came in whistling. Was this the murderer? wondered Dave Smart. Could anyone commit a brutal murder and appear quite so cheerful and carefree?

'Sit down, Richard,' he said.

Then, after the tape recorder had been turned on, he pushed over the photofit picture. 'Have you seen this man?'

223

'Oh yes, he was here yesterday morning, early, soon after nine o'clock.'

'Can you tell us as much as possible about that?'

'Funny, really. He knew my name and asked for me, don't know who'd told him. Then he asked a lot of questions about Barley Hall, about the job. We're supposed to be co-operative and polite with the public, but they aren't usually like this man was. Determined.'

'Go through it for us as far as you can remember.'

'Was he a suspicious character, then? Is he a suspect?' asked Rick brightly.

'We don't know, yet. We're investigating his movements. Probably nothing out of order at all,' replied Dave. 'Did he tell you his name?'

'No, nothing like that.'

'Where he'd come from?'

'He said he was up from London for a day or two and couldn't miss visiting such an interesting project as Barley Hall.'

'Mmm. We did already think he might be from London. Thanks, Rick. That confirms it. If he was telling the truth, of course. Then what? What else did he say?'

'It was funny, really. He asked whether chimneys had been in use at the time Barley Hall was built, and I said no. Then he said weren't there any at all, and I said there was a chimney stack in the newer section at the back, and he asked if he could see it.'

'Very odd.'

'I thought it was funny. People don't usually ask such specific questions. Anyway, I didn't see as he could do any harm, and we can't get on much at the moment so I had time to take him to see the chimney if that was what he wanted. He couldn't do any damage as I could see.'

'True.'

'He ought to have had a hard hat on. Is that what all this is about?'

'No. Though he shouldn't have come on site at all, the public are banned at present. How did he manage it?'

'I thought he must have got permission off someone. I don't know how he got in.'

'Well, we'll leave that.'

'He seemed like someone official, as if he had a right to be on site.'

'Right. Did you take him to see the chimney stack?' went on Dave Smart.

'Yes. He had to climb up the ladder, and he's an old chap, but he managed it all right. The chimney stack is at the back of the Great Hall, and on the first floor there are two openings, fireplaces, only there's no grates in them or owt of that. It was the openings he wanted to see. Said he was very interested in historic buildings, particularly fireplaces.'

'When you got there, to the fireplaces, what did he do?'

'Do?' The carpenter looked nonplussed for a

225

minute. 'He stood and looked at them, both sides of the stack. There's one each side, if you haven't been up there. Then he asked if they had been in good nick when we discovered them, like, during the dismantling of the old building. I said, much the way they are now. He said, was the brickwork in good condition. I said, some of it needs repointing and that, but I'm a carpenter, you'll have to ask the brickies. He sort of fiddled around a bit, tapping the wall. I said, some of them bricks is loose, please don't fiddle around with them, sir, I've showed you the chimney stack and the fireplaces. Then he smiled, all charming, and said he was grateful.'

The carpenter came to a stop.

'And I hope he gave you something for your trouble,' said Dave Smart.

'Well, he did, yes.'

'Thank you, Richard. Did he go after that?'

'He went straight away.'

'Do you remember what time it was?'

'About half-past nine, as near as I can remember. Might have been a bit later. I don't wear a watch for work. I can hear the Minster chimes while we're working here.'

'You've been very helpful about that query. Now, there's something else. Do you want a break for a cigarette or anything?'

'I don't smoke, thanks, but I could do with a Jimmy Riddle.'

*　　*　　*

'What else do you want to ask me, then?' asked the carpenter when they were once more assembled round the architect's table.

'We aren't satisfied about your movements on Wednesday last week between nine o'clock and midnight.'

'Oh no, not that again!'

'I'm afraid so. I have here your answers to our questionnaire...'

*　　*　　*

Elsewhere in York the scene of crime officers had been making a careful search of the skip which had for a short time been such a prominent and objectionable feature of Stonegate. As they didn't know what they were searching for, it was not easy. They knew the basic facts of the murder better than anyone, but inevitably had not kept up with all the paper-work which had been steadily mounting. Nor was it expected that they should.

On top of the skip was a thin layer of rubbish which had accumulated while it was standing in Stonegate. They removed this and set it on one side after a quick examination. Then they were down to builder's rubble. They took this off bit by bit, creating a large pyramid on the floor beside the skip. Much of it they felt they could dismiss out of hand, pieces of wood, half-bricks, scraps of insulation, part-sheets of plastic. They knew the fight which led to the death had first been with hands and secondly with a knife, and that the fall which terminated matters had been apparently straightforward. The victim had not been tripped up by a piece of wood, smothered with a piece of plastic, or any of the other gruesome possibilities which a criminal mind might envisage, when looking at the contents of the skip.

They sifted the dust, which existed in plenty, but found nothing at all suggestive of evidence for a crime.

Then they went through everything again.

After that they rang the incident room and asked if one of the DIs would like to come down to see them, before they disposed of anything. However much they might want, as a matter of principle, to keep the whole contents, it didn't seem necessary.

'I'll go,' John Rollo said. 'Mr Smart is still interviewing, isn't he? But he's on the premises, you can get hold of him if you want him. I'll go down.'

To tell the truth he was glad to get out of the incident room for a bit. There were quite a few people working in there and several machines going, and Rollo preferred to be in the open air whenever he could, no matter what the weather.

'We've asked the forensic scientist to come

as well,' the soco greeted him when he arrived.

'Brian?'

'Yes.'

'That's good. It will be as well to have his opinion. I don't know that I'd want to make the decision on my own.'

They waited around a few minutes, and Brian arrived. The scene of crime team went through the procedures they'd used.

'I think we can certainly discard the builder's waste,' said Rollo, and after some discussion Brian agreed.

'What were you hoping to find?' he asked. 'A bloodstained knife?'

'You never know, with murderers,' replied Rollo. 'They do daft things. I wouldn't put it past them to throw the knife away in a nearby skip. Typical. Most murderers are a bit stupid.'

'That's how we catch them,' one of the scene of crime team said.

'So, you haven't found it,' said Brian.

'As I understand it,' Rollo went on, 'the skip was full of builder's rubble and sweepings by knocking-off time on the evening of the murder. It was delivered at teatime, after the pedestrian-only period, filled up straight away, and it should have been collected next morning before ten, to be emptied. So the only hope of finding anything among the bottom stuff was if the murderer had thrown it in when leaving the scene and it had drifted down to a lower level—or been pushed down, out of sight.'

229

'That's true.'

'All the bottom stuff appeared pristine—what I mean is, just as it was left at knocking-off time, whenever that was that evening. No weapon. No shoe with bloodstains. Nothing at all with blood on it, or anything useful. So we can let it go. We've discovered nothing among that lot that could be used in evidence.'

Once that matter had been settled, they turned to look more closely at the top layer, which had been deposited in the skip after the builders had filled it, during the hours it had been standing in Stonegate unattended.

'Not a very savoury job, yours,' Rollo remarked, pushing a polystyrene tray, which looked as if it had held curry, to one side with his ball-point pen.

'We've kept separately one or two things which looked as if they might have some significance.'

'Well, these don't look as if they have any,' said Brian, who had been inspecting the doormat, the defunct kettle, and various sandwich wrappings.

The set-aside items were mostly small. One or two ball-point pens, which, they supposed, might have fingerprints. Several receipts from various shops. A theatre ticket. Two bus tickets. Several tissues, crumpled. A box of matches and a crushed cigarette packet. A wrapping from chewing gum.

By now a slight depression had settled over the company.

'That's odd,' said Brian, turning something over with his tweezers.

'What's odd?' Half a dozen heads turned in his direction.

'This theatre ticket.'

'Someone walking back to their car after the performance chucked it in, I suppose.'

'You might well think so. But these are Theatre Royal tickets. And the Theatre Royal is dark at the moment.'

'Dark?' enquired someone who only ever watched the telly, and that not much.

'Dark. It has closed for refurbishment, as media people delight to call it, until May. In theatre parlance, *dark*. No lights. The lure of the footlights, the roar of the crowd. None of that. You're sure this lot were all from the top of the skip?'

'Certain. Absolutely. We picked them off carefully and put them over here. Later when we went through them we separated what seemed to be quite useless for the enquiry and that left these things. Definitely right off the top of the skip, along the front edge which was easy for the public to get at, it stuck out into the middle of the road, and the front part of the sides.'

'No chance it could have been at the bottom of the skip, left from the last time it was hired out?'

'It would have got filthy,' put in Rollo.

The theatre ticket was as clean as any theatre ticket could be which had spent a number of

231

hours on top of a skip.

'They've started using computers for issuing theatre tickets,' said Brian, whose wife dragged him to the performances whenever she could. 'They're quite informative. And another thing, they don't take them off you any more and give you half back. You remember they used to be little pale papery things, torn in two across the middle by the usherettes?'

'So do you keep the whole thing?' asked one of the scene of crime team.

'Yes. Exactly like this. There's a whole lot of information on them. Name of purchaser, address, price, booking reference, part of theatre, row and number of seats, name of play, date of performance, time of day of performance, and some mysterious letters and numbers along the bottom. That's all printed on when the tickets are sold. All that's on there beforehand is the logo on the right—not really a logo—name, York Theatre Royal, and telephone number.'

'So this is an old ticket. On the pavement. Some tidy person's picked it up and put it in the skip.'

'Have you ever seen anyone do that? Ever done it yourself?' asked Brian.

Nobody admitted to such public-spirited behaviour.

'The city authorities keep the streets swept, don't they?' someone asked, and John Rollo replied, 'They're very conscientious, particularly about the city centre where all the tourists see it if there's a lot of litter.

'So what date is that ticket?' he went on to ask Brian.

'The fifteenth of February 1992.'

'It would have been swept up, if it had been lying on the street, long before now,' John Rollo said with conviction. 'On Stonegate of all places.'

'Well, we can always ask its owner if he knows how it came to be here. It was issued to one Mr J. Henniker of Heslington.'

'What!' shouted Rollo.

'That rings a bell, does it?' asked Brian.

'Does it say how many people—how many seats—it's for?'

'Two. It's actually in three parts. The first part with the name and address of purchaser, then two sections showing the row and number of the two seats concerned. Actually one long strip, but folded into three parts.'

'By hell,' said John Rollo. 'If only the theatre hadn't been dark. If only it had been for a performance that Wednesday night.'

'I may be wrong, we can check, but I think it's for the last night before it went dark. The performance was *A Slice of Saturday Night*.'

'Ring the theatre,' said Rollo to the scene of crime team. 'There's bound to be someone answering the phone if they've got the builders in.'

'Rewiring, I think,' said Brian.

'Whatever they're doing, if there are tradesmen there, they'll need to be in telephone contact, and surely they will want someone to tell people who ring wanting to book that they're closed at the moment.'

'What do we want to know?'

'If the fifteenth of Feb was the last performance before the theatre went dark.'

One of the team went off to check on this.

'Not that the information will really help us,' went on Brian, whose mind was working like a train. 'Why did you shout out when you heard the name, John?'

Rollo answered, 'Jack Henniker shares a house with Eliot Lleyn, who was a colleague of the victim. So far we've no reason to suspect Lleyn. The three men knew each other, but not very well, apparently. Lleyn and the victim both studied archaeology at York University and Henniker read architecture. Without checking, I can't remember the exact details of the interviews we've had with them.'

'Coincidence, this ticket?'

They both thought about that.

'If it had been for Wednesday night last week ... If only the theatre hadn't been dark ... but as it is, I can't see that it can have any relevance.'

'Which begs the question, how did it get on the skip?'

'There must be a thousand ways for a bit of litter to get into a skip.'

It was like a thorn in their flesh. Each of them knew that they would be unable to think of anything else until this little fact was somehow reconciled with the other facts which surrounded this case.

So the scene of crime team were left to dispose of the pyramid of builder's waste, and to carefully preserve the small debris in evidence bags, with the ticket in a bag on its own.

*　　　*　　　*

Dr Ralph Reiver had dropped in at the incident room. He was surprised not to find Bob Southwell there, but DI Smart explained.

'I wish him well,' said Reiver. 'When does he come back?'

'Tomorrow night, late I expect. We will see him Saturday morning.'

'He'll be at work then?'

'Yes, he said so. Is there anything we can do, Dr Reiver?'

'No, no. I was only going to try to discover how the case was going. It's a big strain for everyone involved. Poor George's parents, his girlfriend, all his colleagues at work, it must be very trying for all of them. Mr Southwell asked me to keep an eye on Miss Beans, and I know she's under a lot of strain.'

'We were all very interested in the story she turned up, about the murder here centuries ago.'

'Yes. She's finished the writing she was doing. It helped her, I think.'

'Would it help her if I asked her to do some research for us?'

Reiver paused, then said slowly, 'I suppose it might. But what, and why?'

'It may be nothing. We seem to have the trail of a precious object but there is a break in its history. If we knew something about Barley Hall in late Tudor to early Jacobean times, it might help us bridge the gap in the evidence.'

Dave Smart felt that it was best at the moment not to go into more detail. The idea that the reliquary which was stolen in 1483, the story Sophie had uncovered, might be the cause of a murder in the twentieth century was too far-fetched for him to tell any lay person about it. Yet all the personnel who had been present when Bob Southwell read out the story of the medieval theft had become convinced that there might be a link—Dave himself wouldn't put it any stronger than that.

'Can you date the period more exactly?'

'Shall we say 1590 to 1610?'

'And what do you want to know?'

'Please don't mention that there is any specific object we are interested in. That might bias her search. If you could say that her previous work has helped us to understand Barley Hall itself and what is involved, and that is helpful—would that be adequate? Then

236

you could say that the back range of building, behind the Great Hall, which was built between approximately those dates, may have some significance for us and we would like to know more about its history...'

Dave Smart was aware that from the normal police-work point of view, this was a load of rubbish, but he was also aware that neither Dr Reiver nor Sophie Beans knew enough about police work to realize whether it was or not.

'So anything she could pick up about Barley Hall between those dates might be of interest?'

'It certainly would.'

'And might help?'

'That too.'

'I'll mention it to her.'

'Thanks.'

*   *   *

When John Rollo arrived back in the incident room the two men had a lot to catch up on. Jenny Wren made them two mugs of tea, as they had missed the normal afternoon brew-up, and they settled down in a corner by the window where they could lean their elbows on the sill and look down at the sauntering passers-by. The normal buzz of conversation and computers in the room was enough to blank out their quiet voices from the rest of the staff present.

Rollo was obviously bursting with his news,

but all the same he asked Dave Smart to go first with his.

'How did you get on with the carpenter? Is he really a suspect?'

'He still is at the moment. He was open and helpful about the man in the brown jacket, but close as an oyster about what he was doing on the Wednesday night. Everything he said was so vague, it was infuriating. At last he said he'd been half-drunk and couldn't really remember, and was so smug about it that I could have thumped him.'

'Difficult to disprove.'

'It's that all right. There are witnesses to him having been in two pubs early in the evening, so he might well have been half-drunk as he says, and not remember. Only he wasn't, I'm damn sure of that.'

'But you believe him about the man DCI Southwell asked us to find out about?'

'He convinced me there.'

'And wasn't holding back some of the truth?'

'I don't think so. So what progress with the skip, then?'

Rollo swigged his tea and let out a long sigh.

'Something and nothing,' he said.

He recounted the contents of the skip conscientiously, before coming to the items which, it seemed, might be significant.

'I've listed them,' he said.

'One or two ball-point pens. Several receipts

from shops. A theatre ticket. Two bus tickets. A box of matches and a crushed cigarette packet. A wrapping from chewing gum.' Dave Smart read through the list himself. He passed it back to Rollo and waited.

'The thing we thought was significant was the theatre ticket,' and Rollo then explained why. 'Except that it doesn't make sense.'

'There's something else of significance,' Dave Smart said.

'Yes? Is there?' Rollo stared at the list.

'The theatre ticket was bought by J. Henniker, right? Same address as Jack Henniker at Heslington.'

'Yes.'

'The boss told me about the interview he had there with him and Eliot Lleyn. He was really annoyed because this Henniker chappie chewed gum non-stop the whole time.'

'The chewing-gum wrapper!'

'I think we'd better get his fingerprints and go over that little lot.'

'Too right, cobber,' said John Rollo.

CHAPTER THIRTEEN

Meanwhile the report John Clark had written, after his day on the team dealing with the new questionnaire, was still in the incident room together with the reports from other members of the team. Early on Friday morning, DIs Smart and Rollo, both keen as mustard to crack the case that day, before Bob Southwell came back from his two-day assessment, had the theatre ticket on their minds first and foremost and the carpenter Richard taking second place; the reports were much lower in the list of priorities.

*   *   *

Dr Reiver had rung Sophie Beans late the previous afternoon and explained that the detectives would much appreciate more knowledge about the buildings which had become Barley Hall, during the period 1590 to 1610.

'But that's Tudor, and early Jacobean,' Sophie had objected.

'So?'

'So, you know that I'm a medievalist, Dr Reiver—Ralph,' she said. 'It's not my period. How can I do anything useful on that period in five minutes? They are bound to think I can get information straight away.'

'You read early scripts rapidly, Sophie. They have set limits, after all. Twenty years.'

'Twenty years of York City Records! That's what it means, Dr—Ralph. You know they are voluminous, and if I want to research on Mondays or Fridays when the City Archives are closed I need to make special arrangements. They're very good and co-operative but it's Thursday now, nearly closing time.'

'Do what you can, my dear. Now I must go. I have a group of students coming for an hour and they'll be arriving in a few minutes.'

Sophie, standing on the landing by the communal phone, gazed at the blank wall in front of her without having the faintest idea how she was going to be helpful to the police in this. She couldn't understand, either, why they wanted to know.

Unfortunately it wasn't late-night opening at the central library—both lending and reference would close at five thirty. She threw on her jacket and, since the spring evenings were cold, put on a scarf and gloves and dashed down Bootham like a mad thing. When she arrived at the main library, after visiting the City Archives, she asked the librarian at the enquiry desk in the lending section what was available on Tudor or Jacobean York.

'Not much, I'm afraid,' she was told. After a few minutes searching, the helpful girl found a copy of a book called *Tudor York*, and Sophie took it out. Then she went upstairs to the reference library with quarter of an hour left, where they also suggested *Tudor York*, and then found her a little stack of some six books which might or might not have something helpful. For ten minutes she was able to sit and look through them, finding the brief sections

241

which were of use to her and making almost unreadable notes. At least at the end of the time, when they were closing and she had to go, the useful books were sorted from those of no use, and the few notes she had made had started her mind working on this new track. It was lucky that she had been able, at such short notice, to make special arrangements to visit the Archives on Friday morning.

So she went home again, carrying the one book on Tudor York, actually quite aided by the sudden request from the police. Sorting through George's files was making her so unhappy she had been finding it hard to continue. Now she had a legitimate reason for putting them out of her mind for a while, and after all, it was flattering that her research was useful. She sat up burning the midnight oil, reading about Tudor York, and by the time DIs Rollo and Smart were conferring on the Friday morning she had begun to have ideas about which records to look at in the Archives, thinking she might visit the Borthwick Institute also for a look at some parish records.

* * *

'I'll go out to Heslington and take their fingerprints, both Lleyn and Henniker,' DI Rollo volunteered.

'We can ask them to come in,' objected Dave Smart.

242

'I'd like to meet them and get an idea of their set-up.'

'Well, phone them first. They might both be out then you've a wasted journey. We can fetch them from work if necessary.'

Jack Henniker was working at home and answered the telephone, so Rollo was soon on his way out of the incident room. He returned with the fingerprints, and the work of checking the debris from the skip to see if they could be matched began immediately.

'How did he react?' asked Dave.

'Antagonistic.'

'That's what I would have expected from the boss's impression of him.'

'Shall we say a certain arrogance?'

'Surely has.'

'He was very het up about our investigations altogether. The next-door neighbour, a lady who lives on her own apparently, had told them we've been enquiring about persons seen going to their house. He's furious. Talking about police states and Big Brother.'

'The boss's new questionnaire!'

'Yes. Has anything been found out by that? Any more sightings of the man in the velvet jacket?'

Dave picked up a neat pile of typed reports. 'Haven't had time to go through them yet. I'll do them now while we're waiting. Don't know what bee the boss had got in his bonnet—he called it a hunch.'

243

Dave quietly settled down to read the reports. It was still only half-way through the morning, and Jenny Wren brought him a mug of coffee. He looked up at her, and their fingers touched as he took the hot drink. For a few seconds they both forgot everything except that they were in love, and once again they had the opportunity during the working day to exchange a look and touch briefly. For both of them this case, with Jenny working so closely with the detective branch, had been illumined by these stray looks and touches. Dave smiled up at her and whispered, 'See you later,' and she nodded slightly. Everyone in the force knew about them, but at work they tried not to let it be obvious. All the same, she went back to her computer in a cloud of radiance, and he gazed down at the reports he was reading as though the sun was in his eyes.

The first few were negative, and although quick to read, very boring. It was not until he looked at John Clark's report that Dave Smart sat up and began to take notice.

'Dr Wrench arrives home from work at about four thirty,' John Clark had written, 'so I timed my visit to coincide with that. He welcomed me in and offered a cup of tea which I accepted and we sat in the kitchen, which overlooks the house Lleyn and Henniker live in. I showed the photofit to Dr Wrench and he recognized the man at once. He agreed that the description was correct. He had seen the man on Tuesday afternoon when he arrived home. The taxi was waiting outside Lleyn's house and the passenger was the man. He got out of the taxi when he saw Dr Wrench arrive and asked him if he knew when Lleyn and Henniker would be in. Dr Wrench thought they would arrive within the next hour, and the man said he would wait and sat in the taxi. Dr Wrench saw him sitting there during the next half-hour and then forgot him. He guesses the taxi finally left at about six thirty, because he remembers thinking it would be a big bill.'

Dave blinked in surprise and read the report again. Then he noticed there was a postscript overleaf.

'Dr Wrench said he had remembered something about the Wednesday evening of the murder. I previously reported that the victim had visited Lleyn's house at about nine thirty that evening and appeared to let himself in, remaining in the house until about ten o'clock. Dr Wrench told Lleyn, when Lleyn returned at ten thirty or ten forty-five, that the victim had been there.

'He now says that he believes Lleyn and Henniker went out again within minutes of their arrival, because his wife reminded him that headlights swept across the closed curtains of the sitting-room, which also faces Lleyn's house, at about 11 p.m. The headlights moved as Henniker's headlights do as he drives out of the garage. Dr Wrench explained that the car

245

belongs to Jack Henniker and he always drives it.'

'How on earth did we miss seeing the importance of John Clark's first report?' wondered Dave Smart. He looked around. No Rollo. Of course, he was at Fulford with the scene of crime officers, checking for fingerprints, or watching them check for fingerprints. Dammit, this was important. He'd have to confer with Rollo immediately. Getting up and walking out, with a quick word to the sergeant in charge of the clerical personnel to say where he was going, Dave left behind him a barely touched mug of morning coffee.

*　　*　　*

Sophie Beans was rather late going for lunch at King's Manor. She doubted if Dr Reiver would still be there. Before collecting her lunch she went into the Senior Common Room, and there he was, sitting chatting to another lecturer.

'May I speak to you later?' she asked, when Reiver noticed her.

'Shall I leave,' asked the other man, 'if you want to talk?'

'No, please,' and Sophie reached out a hand as if to push him back into the chair—he was half rising. 'I haven't had lunch yet. If you are staying for a little while, Dr Reiver.'

On this occasion he did not ask her to call him Ralph, only smiled and said, 'Of course, Sophie, I'll still be here. Don't rush your meal.'

When she had eaten a swift and rather small lunch, she returned to the SCR and sure enough, Reiver was still there, and still talking to the same man. By now the man had risen and was standing as if about to walk briskly away. In a couple of minutes, it was Sophie who was sitting in the chair next to Dr Reiver's.

'How are you getting on?' he greeted her. 'I don't suppose you've had time yet to more than scratch the surface.'

'There is such a thing as beginner's luck,' she answered.

'I notice the subdued glow.' He smiled again. 'You have discovered something.'

'Well, not knowing what they are after, it might be no use at all, but I did find something about Barley Hall, or at least, the buildings on that site, and it is rather astonishing.'

'You're dying to tell me.'

She laughed, and this surprised him. True, it was only a low chuckle, but after all the distress of the last days it was like the gleam of sunshine after a storm.

'Yes, I am dying to tell you. I've been boning up on Tudor York like mad since you rang yesterday, getting the general picture, and all this morning I've been looking at the original city records.'

'Go on. I could never bear suspense.'

247

'I intended to start with 1590 but the later records arrived first so I started with those, not thinking it would matter. Beginner's luck it certainly was. There was a most dramatic incident in 1604, when the range at the back of the medieval hall was being built. It would never have been on record if one of the people involved hadn't made a complaint to one of the aldermen.

'The complainant was a Mark Conisby, a journeyman builder, working for a freeman called Thomas Chew. Thomas was an expert at building chimneys and he was busy with walls and brickwork. Mark had nothing to do so he'd been set to demolish the outer wall of a single-storey structure that had probably been a kitchen. The new building was to cover part of the same ground and the new outer wall was already built. Anyway, while Mark was demolishing this wattle and daub wall he found something made of gold, it's not clear what it was, embedded there. He shouted out in surprise and Thomas Chew came down from the upper storey, where he was finishing a fireplace opening, to see what was up.'

'Yes?'

'Thomas Chew said anything that was found was his, and he grabbed this gold object from Mark Conisby. Then they fought for it and Mark said he was cruelly beaten and bruised by his master. He was in fear of his life. Thomas kept the gold thing. Mark went straight to the alderman and said, "I will be revenged on him, I will see him sat in the stocks, I will pull his ears, I will hang my pennieworth on him and make a divell on him."'

Sophie paused for effect and Ralph Reiver said, 'This is astonishing, Sophie.'

'Isn't it? But that wasn't the end of it...'

Reiver didn't seem to hear this because he was already going on to say, 'There is something made of gold concerned in today's Barley Hall affair, the police bel—'

'Have they decided to make it public at last?' cried Sophie, interrupting.

'Make what public?'

'I don't know much about it, but I was told in confidence months ago that something very precious had been found and the find would be revealed when the time was right.'

Dr Reiver stared at her.

'Why haven't you mentioned this?'

'Why should I? Isn't that what you are talking about?' She looked taken aback.

'It's the crime I'm talking about, George's murder at Barley Hall. Didn't you know that a precious object is believed to be involved in this crime?'

'How could I know? How on earth could I know?'

He thought, she's quite right. This is police knowledge only. I've just picked it up by chance, and shouldn't have mentioned it, let alone taken it as proven. Apparently the police

249

aren't convinced, themselves. But he had stopped listening, and Sophie was talking. He tuned in again.

'I didn't know that anyone outside those immediately involved knew about it. I promised never to say a word. Although I did ask George a few weeks ago when they were planning to reveal it.'

'You did?'

'Yes, but he didn't seem to know.'

'Sophie, Mr Southwell is back tomorrow. I think you must tell him all you know about this.'

'About the Tudor discovery? Of course, I'm looking forward to telling the police. I hope this is the sort of thing they wanted me to find.'

'No. Well, that of course. I'm sure they'll be interested. But what I meant was, you must tell them that you heard of something made of gold months ago, and asked George about it a few weeks since.'

Sophie looked blankly at him, then she said stiffly, 'If the Trust want it kept secret for a while, Mr Southwell will have to ask them. I should never have mentioned it.'

'I shall make an appointment for you to see him in the morning, and you must keep that appointment, my dear, and answer truthfully whatever he asks you.'

'But of course I will be truthful,' said the girl, looking at him with round eyes, more visible than they usually were through the large lenses of her spectacles.

*　　　*　　　*

During the afternoon the police were able to verify that Jack Henniker's fingerprints, and his alone, were on the theatre ticket, a receipt from a music shop, the chewing-gum wrapper and a defunct ball-point pen, all from the skip.

*　　　*　　　*

Bob Southwell reached home late on the Friday night.

Linda had been watching the clock ever since she put the children to bed. She was ready for bed herself, in pyjamas covered by a loose kimono. The children had declared they wouldn't be able to sleep, but when at last she heard Bob's hand at the door they had been absolutely silent for two hours and sleeping peacefully.

Linda jumped up from her chair beside the flickering gas flame-effect fire and almost ran to meet him. Once clasped in his arms she felt safe, secure, as she always did, but she could sense tension running through him. He didn't feel like a happy or confident man.

'Have a good journey, darling?' she asked, reluctant to put the million-dollar question.

'Fine.'

'Hungry?'

'We had an evening meal before leaving. I wouldn't mind a snack for supper, though. And a beer.'

'Relax. I'll get something.'

She hummed a tune quite loudly as she cut a round of sandwiches and prospected in the fridge for a can of beer. When she took it into their through room he was sitting by the fire, gazing into the flicker of the flames.

'Thanks,' he murmured, and she decided to ask nothing until he had eaten. She picked up the jersey she was knitting for Paul and got on with it, checking which row she was on from the pattern.

At last, when he had been finished for some time and hadn't spoken, she said, 'I think it must have been a rather intensive assessment. You seem tired out.'

'That's partly driving.' There was another silence. He got up and put on some music.

'You want to know, don't you?' he said after a while, by which time she was nearly crazy with curiosity. 'Well, we won't know until tomorrow.'

'Tomorrow! I don't believe it!'

'The competition was pretty keen, love. I did all right, but I don't think I did great, as they say.'

She was so disappointed that she could hardly speak, but at last she pointed out that people often think they've done worse than they have in tests and exams. 'What was the opposition like?' she asked. 'You said hardly anything on the phone.'

'Tough. Half a dozen of us, from all over the country. Of course they all thought I'd got it made, being from the area, but it doesn't work like that. I've been thinking, coming home, how I would like to work for the others, and the answer was, not much.'

'You didn't really like them, then?'

'Oh, they were fine as chaps. Bosses, well, that's different. There was only one I didn't seem to get on with as a person—he is from Sheffield. If I don't get it, I hope he doesn't either.'

'You stand as much chance as anyone.'

'Yes, sweet. They're deliberating tomorrow. They will be ringing the chief with the decision as soon as. We should know by tomorrow night.'

She now sat by his feet on the fluffy fireside rug. Her flowery silk kimono had fallen open, showing the peach-coloured pyjamas he specially liked. Talking stopped, and a warm silence took its place. She leaned her head on his knees and he stroked her hair. It was a deliciously relaxing way to end the day and they did not want to break it. Linda was hoping neither of the children chose that time to wake and want something.

'Bed,' she said at last, jumping to her feet and turning off the gas, then the music centre. 'You're falling asleep.'

They walked up the stairs side by side with their arms round one another, Bob stumbling slightly on the turn where he had to cope with the short end of each step.

*　　　*　　　*

Sophie Beans also went to bed. Her spirits had been wildly variable ever since her talk with Dr Reiver, and she was dreading the interview with Mr Southwell the following day. Convinced she would not sleep a wink all night, she fell deeply asleep as soon as her head touched the pillow. It was hours before she began to dream, and at first her dreams were pleasant, even comforting.

She dreamed that she was sitting on a half-demolished wall drinking thin beer out of a horn beaker and listening to an old woman who was reminiscing of the time when she was young. York was different then, the old woman said. There were many hospitals and homes for the old, poor and sick, where they were well looked after. There were many schools for the children. The city was always full of the sound of bells from the forty churches and the abbey and priories and friaries. There were the Miracle Plays once a year on Corpus Christi Day. There were more people, said the old woman, nodding her head in its white linen mutch. Thousands more people than lived in the city nowadays.

'More are coming, old mother,' said the young man Sophie was identifying with in her dream. 'The ruins are being pulled down to build new houses with the stones. You will see more people coming here to live, I'm sure. York is changing. My master is always busy with his brickwork, and making chimneys.'

Newfangled things, said the old woman, filling up the young man's horn beaker with the thin beer. Smoke never hurt anyone. It is good for you.

Sophie pushed back the woollen cap on her head in the dream to scratch her forehead. It kept off the weather with its flat rim all round but the heat of the day made the head itch. The leather breeches and the jerkin made the body itch, but it was sheer indulgence to scratch, sitting here in the sun.

'Are you working, down there?' came the bad-tempered voice of Tom Chew from the upper storey.

'Just having ten-o'clocks,' shouted back the young man, with cheek in his voice. Sophie heard the voice clearly, and the growl in reply, 'Get on with that wall if you want wages today,' and saw or felt herself—being the young man, Mark Conisby—start again banging down the old wall, the daub crumbling away under the hammer and the wattle, weak with age, splitting, breaking. Then there came the glint of gold in the dried old dung, and at the next blow another clod fell away so that

255

something gleamed bright, bright in the sun and Sophie felt her throat shouting in triumph!

She saw fingers, lean brown fingers scrabbling in the mess that had been a wall and picking out the golden thing. It was diamond-shaped and bright, with engraving on the flat sides that looked like Adam and Eve, father and mother of us all, and angels, and the mother of Jesus with her baby.

Then there was the shadow of Tom Chew leaning over and reaching out, saying, It's mine, whatever is found here is mine, and herself that was Mark crying out, No! Finders keepers! and Tom's fist coming down, then they were rolling together on the floor among the mess from the wall, with Tom trying to prise open Mark's fingers, and all Sophie could see in her dream was the darkness of another body and two bodies struggling together, so that instead of enjoying the sun there was cloth and leather coming between the light and the eyes, and the stink of two bodies, all the various stinks, and they grappled and fought all over the floor of what had once been a back-kitchen, perhaps, long before.

Mark blew out his breath and it entered his master's nostrils and Tom's breath scorched Mark's own face; they fought to and fro and the gold thing was forgotten, left to roll or fall where it would.

At last Mark, who should have been the stronger, owned himself beaten and stood up shaking and crying that he had been cruelly beaten and bruised, and Sophie's head thrashed to and fro on the pillow.

'Go, damn you,' cried Tom. 'I am eaten up with your fleas. It is no wonder you spend your time scratching when you could be working. Take your flea-ridden carcass out of here.'

It was all dark now in Sophie's dream and it seemed inevitable that what had been pleasant and sunlit was now black and hurtful and blending into a nightmare on which she was condemned to ride. She felt herself and saw Mark stumbling and running; the darkness was inward, composed of pain and anger. He went on through lanes so narrow his elbows brushed the walls of the houses on either side, until he reached the house of an alderman who knew his family, and then he could ask an audience and tell of the way he had been treated, and the gold he had found, taken from him.

'You must go back to your master,' said the alderman and Mark cried that he was in fear of his life and would not go back.

Then Sophie was sobbing, wetting her pillow, as in her dream she cried out the words she had copied earlier in the day.

'"I will be revenged on him, I will see him sat in the stocks, I will pull his ears, I will hang my pennieworth on him and make a divell on him,"' but even as she cried out she felt a strange sensation and Mark said to the alderman, I must go home, the beating has made me ill.

Then the dream swirled around as Mark made his way through narrow ways to the bridge over the Ouse river and went across to the church of St John, and so along Norgata to his home, one of the hovels in Hagworm's Nest. All the way he was feeling worse and worse and when he thrust open the narrow plank doorway the scene in the dark hovel spun before him. He clutched the jamb of the door, trying to stay upright and not fall headlong into the room where he could see a still form which had once been his mother, and an old woman said, she is worse, she has died, God rest her soul, it is the plague, they are dying in the next house too, you don't look well, Mark, and Mark felt great pain in his chest and could hardly breathe, felt under his arms and in his groin, feeling the swellings there and suddenly crying out loud in triumph, the greatest triumph yet. He thought he was shouting but to the old woman it was a whisper, as he screamed out, I have won after all, for Tom Chew's body and mine were close as mother and child and I have killed him, I have given him his death for his beating of me...

Sophie woke to black darkness, as black as in her nightmare, but here at least there was a paler rectangle which was her window with the blackness paling to grey. She got out of bed and went to fetch a drink of water, thanking God that she had woken from the dream. Sipping cool water she wondered whether she dare sleep again, but her eyelids drooped and she yawned, then climbed back between the sheets, and drifted off once more.

Then it seemed to Sophie that she saw Tom Chew take up a brick to place it in the chimney stack he was building, and find it heavy so that he who could beat any man at the number of bricks he could lay in a day now wavered up, his hand hardly able to bear the weight, and leaned his head on his other hand, and his legs tottered under him, and he thought, I had best put my affairs in order for I am mortal ill. This golden toy has brought badness with it. Then he took the golden bauble and pressed it in behind the last brick he had strength to lift and turned to go home, to make his will and his peace with God while yet he might.

It seemed long to Sophie before the blackness of nightmare lifted so that she stopped thrashing round in her bed and lay quiet, sleeping more peacefully until dawn came and she woke to see a grey sky with a cool wind blowing.

CHAPTER FOURTEEN

Sophie was dreading her interview with Mr Southwell. Her mind was still full of hazy black areas which she put down to nightmare, dread and depression. As far as possible, while eating muesli and drinking tea, she tried not to think.

* * *

All three of the chief officers in the case, Southwell, Smart and Rollo, had arrived at the incident room at the crack of dawn. If Bob Southwell expected to be quizzed about his two-day assessment, he was wrong. It was obvious the minute he saw his staff that they were bursting with their own news.

'Where is everybody?' he asked. Apart from the three of them the place was empty.

'We gave about half the staff the weekend off,' Dave Smart said. 'They've been working all the hours God sends. And we told the others they could have a late start this morning.'

'Might I ask why?' and Bob didn't sound too pleased about it.

'I think you'll agree we can call off the mass enquiries. Wait till you hear—'

'Who's first then?'

'Chronologically, Dave,' said John Rollo, reluctantly.

260

'All right, then, Dave. Get on with it.' Bob thought that putting Smart and Rollo in joint charge seemed to have worked. They were getting on better than they ever had before.

'You asked us to run a questionnaire about the man in the brown velvet jacket.'

'The dealer in exclusive and expensive antiques.'

'Surely, boss. To sum up, he was seen visiting Lleyn and Henniker on the Tuesday afternoon, by their neighbour, Dr Wrench.'

All sorts of things rushed to the front of Bob Southwell's mind. The fact that the dealer dealt in precious medieval objects. The trail throughout the case of something which might be a medieval jewel. The fact that Eliot Lleyn was a colleague of the dead man's and had been on the Barley Hall site during the whole of the work there. Southwell said nothing, but his face changed, the muscles in his jaw tightened.

'Then he was seen next morning, Wednesday, on site by John here.'

'You saw him Wednesday morning, Rollo? I saw him at the view of an antique sale on Wednesday afternoon.'

'He got on site somehow and asked for the only joiner we haven't got an alibi for.'

'That lad Rick?'

'Who showed him the chimney stack.'

'I don't believe it,' Southwell said softly. 'There's just got to be some amazing object in this case. That bloke must have been checking

261

the provenance.'

'There is. We know that now. Sophie Beans is coming in to be interviewed by you at nine o'clock.'

'Sophie?'

'Dr Reiver made an urgent appointment after talking to her yesterday. She mentioned a find on site of something precious which was to be kept secret until the right time came. She also said that a few weeks ago she had asked the victim when it was going to be made public.'

'My stars!' said Bob. 'Why on earth didn't she say this before?'

'Well, you know, boss, we haven't released our suspicions to the media. They are only theories. She wouldn't know a thing about them.'

'That's right,' Bob said reflectively. 'That first interview on the morning the body was discovered—I sent her to the ladies' loo to recover herself a bit. She heard nothing that was said after that, not that there was anything about a precious object.'

'She's hardly been seen since,' Rollo put in.

'I saw her in her flat, and Sarah Doughty was with her and Mr and Mrs Followes on the Friday afternoon. We hadn't put these suspicions together then.'

'The public don't know anything about the hole behind the brick, or the pressure marks on the hand, or anything,' Dave said.

Bob gave himself a shake.

'You realize we might be putting two and two together and making six?' he asked. 'I think we ought to try to keep this at the back of our minds if we possibly can. None of the evidence we have so far would convince a jury or give us a murderer.'

'There's the skip,' said John Rollo, looking as though he would explode if he didn't get his say.

'Go on, John. About the skip.'

'Let me recap,' said John Rollo, thumping his right fist into the palm of his left hand, then raising his fingers, one by one. 'The skip was delivered after the foot-street was opened to vehicular traffic, late afternoon on the Wednesday. It was as near as possible to the entry to Coffee Yard, and it was empty. At once, the builders on site began to wheel out barrows full of rubbish and put it in. They went on doing this until all the rubbish they had was in, and the skip was full, then they knocked off for the day and went home—about 7 p.m. The skip was scheduled to be removed Thursday morning, before the street was closed to vehicles again. While it stood there various things were put into it. We had a man on duty next to the skip from the discovery of the body to the time we moved it, partly to stop anyone disturbing the contents. This didn't prevent some more rubbish being deposited in the skip, but not much.'

'Didn't he stop people putting stuff in?'

'I asked him. He remembers one of the shops bringing an old doormat, and another shop bringing a worn-out electric kettle, and he didn't see any reason to stop them going on the skip.'

'Fair enough.'

'Anything deposited before the area was guarded must have been between 7 p.m. Wednesday and 12.20 or so a.m., twenty after midnight, Thursday morning.'

'Right. Those times are more exact than we had them before. Quite a while seems to have elapsed before scene of crime checked the skip.'

'Yes, sir. There was a lot to do and the skip was low priority, we didn't actually expect to find evidence in it, but it had to be checked in case.'

'Yes.'

Rollo sketched the discoveries of the scene of crime team, and ended with the theatre ticket, which he produced in its evidence bag.

'This is for the fifteenth of February,' said Bob, sounding puzzled.

Rollo explained about the theatre being dark, and how he had gone for Jack Henniker's fingerprints, and the collection of items on which they were found—the pen, the receipt, the chewing-gum wrapper, the theatre ticket—raising fingers in turn as he ticked off each item.

'He might have walked down Stonegate next

morning and chucked them in,' said Bob, but without conviction.

'As it happened he had stated what he was doing on the Thursday and we had noted it down,' put in Dave.

'He was nowhere near Stonegate?'

'Exactly, boss. And I spent some time yesterday checking his movements on the Thursday and witnesses bear out his statement. In my opinion it's kosher,' said John.

'We already knew he and Lleyn spent Wednesday evening in the pub until ten thirty. We know they went straight home—*vide* their own and the neighbour's statements.'

'The neighbour also says they went out again before eleven.'

'That's right. Which directly contradicts their statements.'

'So if Henniker put those items in the skip, which he must have done himself, it means he must have been in Stonegate between say 11 p.m. Wednesday and 12.20 a.m. Thursday. Now why? Why on earth? Unless...'

It was at this point that the rest of the staff began to arrive.

'Let us,' Southwell said quietly to Smart and Rollo, 'get a search warrant for Lleyn's house. If there *is* an object—it's probably on the Continent or in America by now. But there might be some paperwork...'

'We'll get a warrant, sir.'

'Quiet about it.'

Then Bob Southwell turned to greet the staff drifting in by ones and twos. He put on a bright welcoming face and prepared to answer questions about his two days away.

His mind, though, was in turmoil, shot through by strange emotions and wild ideas. What was it about gold, about even the thought of gold, shaped, engraved, enamelled centuries ago, that made men mad? Even his own brain, which he had thought well balanced and sane, was hungering after the discovery of shining gold. Treasure. Was the longing for treasure in every human being, the discovery of treasure, the glamour of gold?

Rollo went to organize a search warrant.

In a few minutes, when he had the opportunity, Dave attracted his boss's attention.

'Last night Dr Reiver left this for you,' he said, picking up some papers from a desk. 'John and I thought of asking Miss Beans if she would investigate the period between 1590 and 1610 for us. That's when they think the chimney stack was built, if you remember, boss. This is a photocopy of her notes. She came up with another sighting of a gold object.'

Reading the notes, Southwell felt staggered by the fracas Sophie had discovered. It seemed as if every time the golden object appeared in history there was trouble.

'I'm looking forward to seeing that young lady,' he said grimly.

*　　*　　*

Sophie Beans arrived at the incident room promptly at nine on that Saturday morning. She had nothing else to do, except that she was planning to go to the market and buy some vegetables. The soft African basket she usually carried had first appealed to her because it made her think of cabbages.

Bob Southwell decided to interview her in the incident room and have done with it. He invited DIs Smart and Rollo to stay with him, as they had been in on the whole of the case already.

It wasn't coffee time, but Southwell sent the rest of the staff downstairs to Thomas Gent's Coffee Shop to have an extra one on him, and told them not to come back for half an hour. Because the alleyway was closed to the public, the coffee shop was not doing much trade. People could walk that far and stand outside the building and peer up at the crane, but the citizens of York were busy about their Saturday shopping and not taking much advantage of this.

When Bob saw Sophie come into the incident room he felt a protective impulse, in spite of what he'd been told.

'Now, Sophie,' he said gently when they were sitting opposite one another, 'we haven't met for some time, have we?'

'No,' she said, and smiled a little, giving him a candid look from two very beautiful grey eyes, before she dipped her head slightly and all he could see were the tops of her cheeks. He noticed that instead of pale skin, there were purple rings as though she hadn't slept, or was ill.

'We are very grateful for the research you did for us,' he went on.

'That's all right.'

'But I am feeling worried about something else. What's this Dr Reiver has been telling me?' Bob said, again more gently than he had intended to speak to this witness.

'He did make a fuss. I don't see that I can tell you anything. If the Trust want something kept secret, how can I talk about it?'

'I had a word with the director and he says that to his knowledge nothing of precious metal has been found on this site,' said Bob.

'Oh,' she said, and her sweet, rather droopy mouth opened a little and stayed open.

'Just what did you hear, when, and who from?' His voice was suddenly much harder.

'It was some months ago,' she said. 'In fact, last summer, about June. All I heard was that something of precious metal—well, gold—had been found on the site and at present it was being kept secret, but would be made public eventually.'

'Surely you knew that this was contrary to

normal archaeological practice?' Bob said.

'I'm not an archaeologist. Yes, if you put it like that, I suppose it did seem strange, but I didn't really think about it.'

'Who told you?'

Sophie bit her lip. 'Eliot,' she said at last.

'Eliot Lleyn?'

'Yes.'

'How well do you know Eliot Lleyn?'

She looked surprised. 'Pretty well,' she said.

'Under what circumstances did he tell you this?' and as she did not answer immediately, Bob's voice grew much firmer. 'Now then, Miss Beans!'

She looked embarrassed. 'It was pillow talk,' she said.

'What?' Bob almost shouted. After a second's silence, he asked, more quietly, 'Are you telling me you and Eliot Lleyn are lovers? What about George Followes?'

'Oh, it was before George,' Sophie said indignantly. 'Of course.'

'Of course.' Bob tapped on the table. 'Of course, you and Eliot had been lovers before you and George were lovers, and no one thinks to tell me.'

'No one asked how well I knew Eliot,' Sophie said, still rather indignantly.

'How well did George know Eliot?'

'Oh, very well.'

'So this was a pally arrangement?'

'I'm afraid it wasn't like that at all,' Sophie

269

said. 'It was all very distressing and I'd rather not talk about it. I don't like to think about it.'

Bob's voice was much quieter now. 'Tell me, and then perhaps we can forget it. Was it a case of off with the old love, on with the new?'

'No. I was disillusioned with Eliot's character.' Sophie was firm. 'I couldn't go on with him. We all make mistakes, and my relationship with Eliot was a mistake. I stopped respecting him. George wasn't the cause at all. He and I were only friends at the time.'

'You were friends? Until when?'

'Until the autumn, after I'd left Eliot. I was treading slowly in the new relationship, anxious not to make another mistake, I suppose.'

'Did you know that George went up to Eliot's house after leaving your flat on that Wednesday night?'

'Oh no, he didn't, did he?'

'He did. Dr Wrench across the road saw him and spoke to him.'

'He sees in the dark, that man. I expect he was outside fiddling with his motor-caravan.'

'He was.'

'He spends ages fiddling with it,' Sophie said conversationally.

'He saw George go into Lleyn and Henniker's house.' Bob broke off to say, 'You seem to know Dr Wrench's habits very well.'

'I ought to,' said Sophie, 'I lived opposite

him for two years.'

'Which house did you live in?' asked Bob, thinking of the single lady who was Lleyn and Henniker's next-door neighbour. Perhaps she had taken Sophie in as a lodger.

'My own house,' said Sophie. 'Eliot and I bought it between us. Well, we have a mortgage on it, of course. But you were wrong, Mr Southwell, in calling it "Lleyn and Henniker's house". If you want to refer to it like that, it should be "Beans and Lleyn's house".'

Bob didn't know what to say.

Dave Smart and John Rollo didn't know what to say either. They looked at one another.

Sophie broke the silence. 'Eliot had some capital and my grandmother left me some money when she died.'

'You are telling me, Sophie,' Bob said, 'that when you and Eliot Lleyn were lovers you bought a house together?'

'It's not unusual, nowadays,' replied Sophie. 'We thought we were permanent.'

'No, of course it is not unusual. It would have been helpful if we had known.'

'Everybody knew,' Sophie said. 'It wasn't a secret. Then it happened that George started working with Eliot and became friendly and started coming round all the time. That was last summer. After a while ... well ... like I said, I walked out on Eliot and got a flatlet, I'd have done that anyway, I couldn't stand living

271

with him any longer ... and he and George had the most awful bust-up. In fact there were so many quarrels last summer. It was horrible. I was glad when it all calmed down. George and I weren't lovers until everything had calmed down.'

'But you still own half the house?'

'Houses haven't been selling recently, with the economic recession. Obviously it will have to be sold, when things start moving again. Then we will split the money between us, Eliot and I.'

'I mentioned a few minutes ago,' a shattered Bob went on, 'that George had gone into the house—the house you and Eliot Lleyn own between you. How do you think he was able to do that?'

Sophie heaved her soft basket from the floor on to her lap and found her small handbag in it. She scrabbled in the handbag and brought out a key-ring and looked at it.

'He took my key,' she said flatly.

'George took your key on the Wednesday, before leaving you at nine o'clock?'

'He must have done. It isn't here. The back door key is, but not the Yale for the front.'

'Why, do you think, did he go up to Heslington that Wednesday night?'

'Well, it wouldn't be to see Eliot,' Sophie said, 'because he and Jack always play darts in a pub on Wednesday nights. They're in the darts team and if they aren't practising they're playing matches.'

'Isn't that a rather down-market hobby for people like Lleyn and Henniker?'

Now it was Sophie's turn to look surprised. 'I hadn't thought about it like that. It's just something they are good at. Sign of a misspent youth, George used to call it,' and she looked as though she would break down into a weep.

'Now, don't cry, Sophie,' Bob said quite sharply. 'We haven't finished this yet. You never told us there was animosity between George and Eliot, over you.'

'Over me? I suppose it was. But it shouldn't have been, because I didn't break with Eliot because of George. Anyway, the animosity was finished. And no one ever asked me anything like you've asked me this morning.'

'Eliot said he and George didn't move in the same social circles.'

'They don't now,' said Sophie. 'I mean they didn't—after all the rows.'

'And you, according to Dr Reiver, mentioned to George a few weeks ago the precious something that had been found?'

'I only asked George when news of it was going to be released. He said he hadn't heard of anything like that being found. I said maybe I'd misunderstood. He said who'd told me; I said, Eliot. That was rather awkward, because of course, we never mentioned Eliot. Then he didn't speak of it again, and I forgot about the whole thing.'

'So when George was killed, you never thought of his quarrels with Eliot, or the find which was being kept secret?'

'No, of course not. Whatever could that have to do with it?' asked Sophie.

'You told us you thought he was keeping something from you during those last few weeks.'

'That was the feeling I had.'

'It didn't occur to you that the golden object Eliot Lleyn had told you about might be preying on George's mind?'

'No! Surely it couldn't have been that!'

'Miss Beans,' Bob said wearily, 'thank you so much for your co-operation. Thank you too for the research you've done for us. It has been most useful in giving us background to this case. Now, I must ask you not to mention this interview to anyone. Anyone at all, even Dr Reiver. You can tell him it has taken place, as he arranged it, and that is all. *Do not* speak of it *at all* to Eliot Lleyn, or to anyone else *at all*. You may go now.'

* * *

The three policemen leaned on the windowsill and watched Sophie emerge from Coffee Yard and then walk towards Davygate and, ultimately, the market.

'Everyone told me she was such a nice girl,' Bob said, wearily.

'She is,' answered John Rollo. 'A very nice girl.'

'"Nobody asked me, sir, she said,"' quoted Dave Smart.

The rest of the police staff came up the stairs from their bonus coffee break.

*　　*　　*

Sophie's head was vibrating with pain. She managed to go round the market and stock up with fresh fruit and vegetables. Then she went into a restaurant which was serving drinks and collapsed into a corner seat. Her thoughts went round like rats in a trap. The nightmare of the previous night was still shrouding her mind with its images, and now the interview with Acting DS Southwell had added a whole lot of new doubts and fantasies.

Could she possibly be responsible for what had happened to George? Only if Eliot was the murderer.

Was she going to become very ill? If so, she didn't want it to be in the middle of York in a restaurant. For the first time she wished that she had taken up Dr Reiver's suggestion and gone home to her parents for a few weeks. How would she fare alone in her flat? Would it be better to go to someone she knew? By now she thought a pile-driver was busy in her temples. But who did she know well enough to collapse on them? Although she had a crowd of friends

275

and acquaintances, turning to someone when in trouble demanded a special level of closeness. Sophie sat on over her tea, feeling by turns faint and sick.

* * *

'We haven't a scrap of evidence against Eliot Lleyn,' Bob Southwell said, 'except that he must have had an animosity against the victim, and that he mentioned a precious object to Sophie Beans last June.'

'If they had fought over Sophie,' John Rollo said, 'surely it would have been at the time of the break-up, not months later.'

'There was the visit of the man in the velvet jacket to Lleyn's house,' put in Dave Smart.

At last they decided to bring in both Lleyn and Henniker and at the same time search the house in Heslington, and see where all that took them.

* * *

In practice, Henniker was the first to be interviewed; he was brought to Coffee Yard and seen in the architect's temporary office. Lleyn, who was viewed more seriously, was taken to the police station.

'We have reason to believe,' Bob stated, 'that you were in Stonegate on the Wednesday night when the murder took place.'

Henniker looked much as he had the last time Bob saw him. Still elegantly nonchalant, still chewing gum.

'Would you mind not chewing gum during this interview,' Bob added, exasperated, waiting for an answer from Henniker. The man took the wad out of his mouth and, with an insolent air, stuck it on an ashtray in the middle of the table. But he was not feeling confident, that much was obvious to a trained observer. The question had rattled him badly, and Bob was not going to reveal how they knew, if he could help it.

'Why should I be?' Henniker answered at last.

'That is what we want to find out,' Bob said. 'We want you to prove to us that you are not the murderer in this case.'

Henniker's confidence dropped by several degrees.

'Of course I'm not,' he said.

'Then you won't mind telling us what you were doing in Stonegate. As you have provided us with an account of all you did on the evening of that Wednesday up to shortly before eleven, when you left Heslington, and as we have witnesses to all of that time, also to your account of where you went on the Thursday morning, you must have been in Stonegate later than—say—eleven, and not later than say twelve twenty.'

'I never left the house after we got back from

the pub,' Henniker said.

'Your neighbour opposite says that you did.'

'Nosy Dr Wrench? He can't have told you that. It's not true.'

'He told us that the victim visited your house earlier that evening and let himself in to wait for you. He told us that when you and Mr Lleyn returned from the pub, he notified you of this visit.'

Henniker squirmed in his seat. He didn't see how he could deny this.

'Cheeky bastard,' he said. 'How would you like it if someone went into your house when you weren't there?'

'So you and Lleyn felt annoyed at this intrusion?'

'We certainly did.'

'What had the victim done during the period he spent in your house—what signs of his occupation did you find? Had he left a note, for instance? Made himself a drink? Anything at all?'

'Things were disturbed,' the man muttered.

'Disturbed? He had been looking for something?'

'That was how it seemed, yes. Like a common thief.'

'Ah, now we're getting somewhere. Something was missing, was that it?'

'I didn't say that.'

'You implied it. Something of value?'

'I'm not saying any more.'

'So, when you and Lleyn found something was missing, you decided to chase after Followes in your car? Was that it?'

Henniker was silent.

'It's in your own interests to tell us,' Bob remarked. 'Don't you want to clear yourself from suspicion?'

'Followes was nothing to do with me,' stated Jack Henniker. 'Hardly knew the man.'

'I seem to remember,' and Bob looked down at his notes, 'that you told me he was a bit of a wimp, always going on about ethics, and your friend Lleyn said he should have had a soap box?'

'Always preaching. When I did see him, yes.'

'That was your impression of him?'

'Yes.'

'So when you found he had entered the house where you were living, in your absence, yours and Lleyn's, you perhaps wished to point out to him that this was not ethical behaviour, was that it?'

'Something like that.'

'You did leave the house?'

'All right, all right, we went after him.'

'You drove Lleyn after him, knowing that he would be on foot and much slower than the two of you in your car. I presume you went down Hull Road. Then where?'

Henniker said nothing.

'What was it that was missing from your house?'

279

'It was just a watch. One of Eliot's.'

'A watch? A gold watch, by any chance?'

'Belonged to his grandfather,' Henniker said.

'So where did you go after George Followes?'

'We went to his digs,' Henniker said. 'But he wasn't there. His landlord spoke to us. He thought Followes had stayed at Sophie's.'

Something else we weren't told, thought Southwell. Caile could have remembered that, one would have thought, instead of being so wrapped up in his own reactions.

'Then what?'

'We only stayed there a few minutes then went home.'

Henniker then demanded a solicitor, so while they were waiting, Bob Southwell decided to check on this visit to Caile's. He sent Dave Smart round to the house in a police car, hoping that as it was Saturday Marius would be at home.

* * *

Dave found Marius Caile on his hands and knees scrubbing out the room he had let to George Followes.

'Not more questions!' Marius exclaimed.

'Only one or two,' replied Dave.

'You may as well come through,' and Marius dried his hands and led the way into the dining-room.

'The night of the murder,' began Dave, 'we understand that your lodger was at Heslington at his colleague's house, leaving at half-past ten to walk back to town again.'

'Well, I don't know anything about that,' said Marius.

'No, I'm putting you in the picture. He seems to have taken something from his colleague's house, which we have been told was a gold watch.'

Marius looked at him and said nothing, so Dave went on, 'Mr Henniker says that he drove Mr Lleyn to this house at around eleven o'clock and that they spoke to you, asking where Mr Followes was. I have come to talk to you about it, because you did not mention this in your statements to us.'

'It must have slipped my mind,' Marius Caile said.

'Rather an important thing to forget, don't you agree?'

'I was getting ready for bed.'

'And a knock came at the door?'

'That's right. There were these two men outside, looking steaming angry and wanting to find George.'

'Then what happened?' Dave could see hesitation. He remembered that this witness had lied to the police in previous interviews. 'We will find out, you know,' he said heavily.

Dave was a big man, active and strong, and

281

he towered over Marius in a dominating manner, and glared at him. Marius's nerve broke.

'All right,' he said. 'They came in. They said George had stolen something and they wanted to look in his room. They thought he could have been back here while I was across at the Brigadier with my pals and put it away and then gone out again. I didn't want them roaming round in there so I said I'd look, if they would wait in here. I went and searched all over but could find nothing unusual and came out and told them so. It didn't look to me as if he'd been back since half-past six.'

Dave Smart remembered that the scene of crime officers had found Caile's fingerprints all over his lodger's room.

'Then?' he asked.

'Then they insisted I went with them. They were looking for George. I don't know what they thought I could do.'

'You went with them?'

'They made me. I wanted to go to bed. It was nearly twenty past eleven by then.'

'Where did you go?'

'Roaming round town. Then we caught sight of George. They parked the car and left me standing with it to stop George if he went that way. But as soon as they were out of sight I walked home. I knew nothing else until next morning.'

'He's lied to us before,' Southwell said when he heard this from Dave Smart. 'Repeatedly. But I'll confront Henniker with this and see what comes of it.'

*　　*　　*

They settled down again, Jack Henniker with a solicitor by his side. Bob Southwell repeated what they had been told by Caile, and Henniker, looking considerably rattled, agreed that was what had happened.

'We drove in the direction of the town centre, then Eliot caught sight of George walking in the direction of Coffee Yard. Well, I wouldn't have thought he was going there, but Eliot did. He got out of the car and told me to wait for him at the Stonegate end. I parked the car and told that bloke to stay by it. I walked down Stonegate. I waited a long time.'

'So you stood at the end of Coffee Yard, next to the skip, waiting for Eliot?'

'Yes.'

'What did you do while you were waiting?'

'Nothing. Walked up and down. Felt worried in case he didn't get it back. Then Eliot came running, and he had got the reliquary back.'

'What?' shouted Bob Southwell. 'What had he got back?'

'Oh—the watch—his grandfather's watch...'

'Go on,' said Bob grimly, with a glance at the solicitor.

'He told me he'd had to fight George for it.'

At that moment Henniker, who had been moving his fingers nervously to and fro in his pocket, withdrew his hand and reached out to drop something in a waste-paper basket which was standing at the end of the table.

Bob stood up, as if casually, and took a few steps round the room. Before he sat down again, he saw that Henniker was scrabbling in his other pocket, while his eyes seemed to be wandering as if he was unable to concentrate on anything. As Bob came back to his seat at the table, he glanced at what had been thrown away. He could see to the bottom of the wastepaper basket without making it obvious. Lying there was a chewing-gum wrapper.

A picture rose in Bob's mind of Stonegate at night; of a tense Henniker walking up and down, then standing next to the skip and gazing down into Coffee Yard, perhaps even hearing the sound of raised voices. His fingers scrabbling in his pocket and fishing out whatever they found there—an old theatre ticket, a couple of tissues, a defunct ball-point pen, a chewing-gum wrapper. He doubted if Henniker was aware of having thrown them away. Judging by the way he had just discarded this wrapper—as if it was nervously

284

compulsive behaviour—he wouldn't even remember. He seemed quite unconscious now of Bob's scrutiny.

Even as Bob watched, Jack Henniker reached out and dropped a crumpled tissue and an envelope into the waste basket.

CHAPTER FIFTEEN

The two detectives who went to search Eliot Lleyn's house under the supervision of Dave Smart set about the task carefully and thoroughly. They had almost given up when one of them, who was moving things about which had accumulated at the bottom of a fitted wardrobe, came across the door to a small safe which had been let into the base.

It was locked, but Dave had noticed a miniature key in one of the drawers of a desk, and it fitted. They all clustered round, silent but tense, and watched as the key turned and the small door, a few inches across, was lifted.

There was only one thing in the safe, and Dave moved it out carefully, surprised at the weight. It was wrapped in tissue paper. He unfolded the paper, and the cause of so much tragedy lay glowing at them.

'What is it when it's at home?' asked Pete in a whisper.

'It's gold, for one thing. Doesn't tarnish,'

said Dave.

'I'd love to hold it,' said the other detective.

'You might be able to after Brian's had it for forensic examination,' Dave said. 'It's what's called a reliquary. That's for putting relics of a saint in.'

Pete wasn't sure what relics were but didn't like to ask.

'It's just like that description the boss read out to us. A white enamel rose with a diamond in the middle, but that pointed thing isn't what I would call a diamond,' said the other detective.

'They perhaps didn't know how to make them sparkle, in those days,' said Dave.

'You can see the figures on either side,' Pete remarked. 'Adam and Eve, did the boss say? I don't think much of her for a Page Three girl.'

The reliquary lay there and brought into the modern room the atmosphere of days long ago; they tried to imagine the centuries between, but the thought made them dizzy. This little thing, to be worth such a lot of money! To have survived, when the world which brought it into being had long gone!

*   *   *

When they reached the incident room with the reliquary, everyone was dying to look at it, Bob Southwell as much as any of them.

'You found it, then? Let's see it!' he

286

exclaimed.

On a central table it was slipped out of its evidence bag and the tissue paper carefully unfolded once more so that they could see the top.

Everyone gathered round and stared.

There before their eyes was the reliquary made of gold, exactly as described in the fifteenth-century records which Sophie Beans had discovered. It gleamed brightly, but not with the glitter of new jewellery in a shop window. It had, though, a presence, a personality which beat most gold objects into a cocked hat. Bob turned it over with tweezers so that they could see both sides.

'There must be two and a half million pounds' worth lying there,' Sarah Doughty said quietly. It was strange how they all found themselves whispering.

'In view of this,' Southwell said after a few minutes to the room in general, 'we'll disband this incident room and move back to Colliergate.'

He was anxious to play out the last scene in the tragedy and confront Eliot Lleyn. His mind was now full of the image of the young archaeologist who had lain, murdered, between the dustbin and the concrete mixer on a cold March morning.

*　　　*　　　*

Southwell walked into the room where Eliot
Lleyn was sitting, and told him he was under
arrest for the murder of George Followes.
Eliot was looking as neat and smart as usual,
and very self-confident. His confidence took a
knock when the reliquary in its evidence bag
lay on the table between them and Southwell
said to the tape recorder, 'I am showing Mr
Lleyn the bag containing the fifteenth-century
reliquary.'

He remembered how Lleyn had persistently
talked about the archaeological background to
the project during interviews instead of talking
about his relationship with George Followes.

Then he asked, 'It didn't strike you that it
was wrong for an archaeologist to steal
treasure from a dig?'

'That's the stuff George was always
spouting. It didn't belong to anybody. Finders
keepers. We weren't hurting anybody by
keeping it. No one was a penny worse off.'

'Someone is dead.'

'You needn't think I'm taking the rap on my
own,' said Lleyn. 'There's four of us in this.'

'You and Jack Henniker?'

'He thought we were going away together,'
Lleyn remarked bitingly, 'to tropic climes. Fat
chance he'd got.'

'So who else?'

'Caile for one.'

'Caile?'

Lleyn laughed. 'Told you we forced him to

288

come with us that night, did he? I thought he might.'

'He says he was left by the car and straight away walked home.'

'He came with me and we found Followes, that stupid idiot. He was on his way to the director's house, was going to rouse him at that time of night, all goody-goody, and give him the reliquary. Give away a fortune!'

'Archaeologists don't steal from digs,' Southwell said again. 'It's against all the ethics of your profession.'

'Ethics! You're as bad as he was. Not that we meant to kill him. All he had to do was give it back and keep his gob shut.'

'What I can't understand,' Southwell said at one point, 'is that what made you steal was greed, what made you betray all the standards of your vocation was greed, what made you kill was greed. Love, I could have understood. Greed, I cannot.'

*　　　*　　　*

Bob Southwell had stopped bothering about the carpenter, Rick. Indeed, he had almost forgotten his existence in the excitement of actually seeing the reliquary and arresting the murderer. But later that morning a quiet, mouselike young woman appeared and asked to see him.

'Rick tells me you want to know what he was

doing on the night of the murder,' she said. 'He was with me.'

'Why didn't he tell me, then?' asked Bob.

'Because I'm married to someone else, that's why. He turned violent and I'm living in a women's refuge at present. Rick's afraid of attracting attention to me, from the police or anyone. I told him he must tell you the truth, and he wouldn't, so I came.'

Bob Southwell was too old a hand to be taken in by appearances, but this girl's gentle movements and candid eyes convinced him she was telling the truth.

'That's one less problem for me, then,' he told her.

'It's all going to be all right, you see,' she went on, 'when he gets the money for that thing he found. Mr Lleyn's arranging it all. Rick's going to get a lot of money. Then we are going to go away together. That thing he found behind the brick.'

*   *   *

In the end Sophie had rung Dr Reiver from the café, and he had come at once and found her there. He in his turn used the café's phone and spoke to the railway station and then to Sophie's mother and lastly to a taxi firm, and in next to no time he had put the girl on a train.

'Your mother's meeting you, Sophie,' were his last words before the train moved off.

'Hang on. You've got those aspirins?'

She nodded, and waved through the window, then flopped back, her basket of vegetables on her knee. It was all going to be all right. Dr Reiver had promised to stop her milk and clear out the fridge. She was going home, and needn't worry about anything any more.

*   *   *

It was late afternoon when Bob Southwell was summoned to the telephone. As soon as he recognized his chief's voice on the line, the thought of the promotion assessments flashed into his mind. The voice was so non-committal Bob couldn't decide whether the news was good or not. Come to his office. Right. He'd do that.

Standing outside the door Bob knew he'd never been so apprehensive in his life. He couldn't stand there for ever. He must knock and go in.

His chief's face was not encouraging. Bob knew then. He would have been all smiles if there'd been good news to give.

'Sit down, Southwell.'

Surely if he'd been successful it would have been 'Sit down, Bob'?

'It's not good news, I'm afraid.'

'Right, sir.'

'They thought very well of you, but they feel you need a little more experience. I'm sorry.'

291

'That's all right, sir. It can't be helped.' After waiting what seemed like minutes but was all of ten seconds, Bob added, 'Is there anything in the nature of a debriefing, sir?'

'You will be receiving some notes on how you did, points to note next time, and of course, praise for what you did well. It will be coming by post.'

Now for what he was dying to ask.

'If I didn't get the post, sir, can you tell me who did?'

'I am really very sorry you didn't get it, Southwell. You had my recommendation. The new super will be Bruno Hallam, from the Sheffield area.'

Bob did his best to hide his resentment and shock. Not Hallam! Not Hallam from Sheffield!

'Oh,' he managed to say aloud. 'I'm sure he'll be very efficient, sir.'

'How did you find him?' Now the worst was over, the chief was more relaxed, more inclined to be chatty.

'Oh, fine, sir.'

'When you've been temporarily in the post it's always hard to give it up and go back to the lower position, but it's character-forming, Bob.'

'Bob' now, Southwell thought bitterly.

'And I must congratulate you on the outcome of this Barley Hall investigation. Very satisfactory indeed.'

292

The chief went on, 'You will still be acting detective superintendent for a while because it isn't possible to release Bruno Hallam for transfer straight away. So you'll be able to wind up this case, Bob.'

* * *

Dr Reiver rang Sophie at her parents' house to tell her the news of Eliot Lleyn's arrest for murder, and three others for lesser charges. Her voice sounded dull and dead, but she assured him she was perfectly all right. She's young, he thought. She's had a shock but she'll get over it.

By the time the trial of the four men came up, she had recovered to a large extent, and stood to give her evidence without a tremor. Her voice by then was calm and clear.

Taking her for lunch during the weeks of the trial, Reiver found that sadness still seemed to pervade her personality. He chatted brightly of the excitement nationwide over the fantastic find of the reliquary in the brickwork of the chimney, and passed on goodwill messages from her friends.

'Everyone wants to know when you are coming back to live in York,' he told her.

'It was hard coming for the trial,' she told him. 'Going to sleep in my flatlet has been even harder. But I am coming back to stay. Please tell everyone that. It was good of you to send

293

George's files down to me. I've started working on those again, and my tutor's arranged for me to have extra time for my own work.'

'Barley Hall has been progressing well,' he told her. 'It's really taking shape. I told the director it will be magnificent, a project well worth the trouble. People will enjoy it immensely.'

The time had not yet come when Sophie could go back to sample the new delights of Barley Hall. York seemed strange when it meant the Assize Courts and the Castle, and the walk from there along the riverside to Bootham and her flatlet.

The memory had stayed in her mind of her own York; at midday, with Big Peter ringing out his long celebration of noon over the busy streets; of the friendly atmosphere of the King's Manor restaurant, and the tree in the courtyard which turned into a golden glory in the autumn; of her research in the fascinating city records; of the happy atmosphere of Coffee Yard and Barley Hall as she had known it, the happiness of an adventure to recreate the past, with everyone working together.

'I'm coming back,' she said firmly.

Dr Reiver smiled in response. He looked, she thought, like a kind of battered eagle. Battered by time and experience, his great shoulders bowed by the weight of the years, his face rather fierce and gaunt yet strangely restful like peace after battle.

*   *   *

At the trial the forensic scientist gave evidence. He had examined the reliquary, which measured 62 millimetres by 33 millimetres and 18 millimetres deep, and was of very pure gold, decorated by engraving, enamel, and precious stones. Inside were the remains of a silk fabric which would have held a small relic, long since decayed away. He thought the reliquary was once hidden in a wattle and daub wall, because round the edges where there was a slight rim, he found dirt which he identified as clay and cow dung. The sides seemed to have become clean with handling, but again he found a trace of dust from old pointing, probably from between bricks, in the deepest engraving. This was consistent with the evidence that it was found bricked up in a chimney stack.

The local paper described it as a most spectacular object. 'Stunning' was the word most used.

*   *   *

In the time that had elapsed between the arrest and the trial, Robert Southwell's last day as acting detective superintendent had arrived. On that day he had spent time clearing the desk in the comfortable office he had learned to like.

Lower in the building, Dave Smart spent his last day as acting detective chief inspector and cleared the desk which would soon be returned to Bob Southwell. Dave was profoundly relieved to be going back to the job of detective inspector. He couldn't clear that desk fast enough.

Southwell stood still at last and looked around the super's office to make sure he'd not forgotten anything. His time here had been harassing, testing, worrying, but he hated having to give up this office and the job to Bruno Hallam of Sheffield.

At least no one could take the triumph of the Barley Hall murder investigation from him.

Once arrived at Fulford police station, Bob joined the row of senior officers on the tarmac.

'Have to make him feel welcome,' his chief remarked. 'He's supposed to be one of the high flyers. We're lucky to get him from what I hear.'

Bob's smile felt sycophantic on his face even as he produced it.

There was an increasing noise from the vast area of sky above them. A helicopter came into view. It spiralled downwards to the area of tarmac as the line of senior officers craned their necks to watch its descent.

Bruno Hallam had arrived.

We hope you have enjoyed this Large Print book. Other Chivers Press or Thorndike Press Large Print books are available at your library or directly from the publishers.

For more information about current and forthcoming titles, please call or write, without obligation, to:

Chivers Press Limited
Windsor Bridge Road
Bath BA2 3AX
England
Tel. (01225) 335336

OR

Thorndike Press
P.O. Box 159
Thorndike, Maine 04986
USA
Tel. (800) 223–2336

All our Large Print titles are designed for easy reading, and all our books are made to last.